Don't miss a single mishap!

Read all the Princess DisGrace adventures:

A Royal Disaster

The Dragon Dance

Princess DisGrace

A Royal
Disaster

Lou Kuenzler

illustrated by Kimberley Scott

Random House 🏠 New York

Text copyright © 2014 by Lou Kuenzler
Illustrations copyright © 2014 by Kimberley Scott
Cover art copyright © 2016 by Sara Not

All rights reserved. Published in the United States by
Random House Children's Books, a division of
Penguin Random House LLC, New York. Originally published in
paperback by Scholastic Ltd., London, in 2014.

Random House and the colophon are registered trademarks of
Penguin Random House LLC.

Visit us on the Web! randomhousekids.com

Educators and librarians, for a variety of teaching tools,
visit us at RHTeachersLibrarians.com

Library of Congress Cataloging-in-Publication Data
Names: Kuenzler, Lou, author.
Title: Princess DisGrace : a royal disaster / by Lou Kuenzler.
Other titles: Royal disaster
Description: First American edition. | New York : Random House Books
for Young Readers, [2016] | Series: Princess DisGrace ; [1] | "Originally
published in paperback by Scholastic UK in 2014." | Summary: Paired
with a clumsy, dirty unicorn, a princess who is neither elegant nor
graceful must prove herself at Tall Towers Princess Academy.
Identifiers: LCCN 2015031376 | ISBN 978-0-553-53775-8 (hardback) |
ISBN 978-0-553-53777-2 (hardcover library binding) |
ISBN 978-0-553-53776-5 (ebook)
Subjects: | CYAC: Princesses—Fiction. | Unicorns—Fiction. | Boarding
schools—Fiction. | Schools—Fiction. | Humorous stories. |
BISAC: JUVENILE FICTION / Humorous Stories. | JUVENILE
FICTION / Royalty. | JUVENILE FICTION / School & Education.
Classification: LCC PZ7.K94876 Pr 2016 | DDC [Fic]—dc23
LC record available at http://lccn.loc.gov/2015031376

Printed in the United States of America
10 9 8 7 6 5 4 3 2 1
First American Edition

To my girls
—L.K.

CHAPTER ONE
Once Upon a Time . . .

A terrible beast was coming.

Huge and hairy, it lumbered down the cliffside.

"Help!" cried the twelve terrified princesses gathered in the harbor below. Tall Towers Princess Academy was far across the waves on Coronet Island, and the dolphins that pulled the golden school boat had seen the raging beast and fled back out to sea.

"Thurr," breathed the shaggy creature, panting heavily as it hurtled down the path.

The twelve frightened princesses clung helplessly together on the shore. They were surely doomed. They would never make it to their new school now. They would never dance in the famous glass ballet studio. Never ride their unicorns through Silver Meadow in the morning dew. Never sleep high up in the tall towers that gave the school its name. Instead, the royal First Years would perish here—eaten alive by the terrible hairy beast.

"Wait till my daddy hears about this," wailed a princess named Precious. She stamped her satin slippers so hard that a shower of hairpins fell from her butter-yellow ringlets.

"Please, remain calm," said Lady DuLac, the headmistress of Tall Towers, who was waiting on the pier with the new girls.

But the princesses began to run wildly in

circles, flapping their dresses and squawking like frightened geese.

The wild monster was covered from head to foot in thick, shaggy brown fur. It was hard to make out any eyes or mouth. Just a terrible shapeless head, nodding as it stumbled blindly toward them.

Someone threw a stone.

"Don't hurt the poor thing," begged a red-haired princess, though her voice was shaking with fear. "It just wants to be friendly. I think it's trying to curtsy. Look."

The creature stopped at the edge of the harbor, wobbling on one leg.

"Greetings," said the headmistress, stepping boldly forward. Her pale blue robes shimmered in the sun, and her long silver hair tumbled like a waterfall to her waist.

"Lesson one, Young Majesties. A princess is always courteous," she said.

She held out a white-gloved hand toward their hairy visitor. "Hello." She smiled. "I am Lady DuLac, the headmistress at Tall Towers Academy. Can I help you?"

The monster bowed its head and growled something from deep inside its shaggy fur. Then it wobbled again and fell in a tangle on the dock.

"Eew," gasped Princess Precious, leaping backward. "It's not a monster. . . . It's . . . it's *human*."

The hairy heap sat up. "Of course I'm human," said a muffled voice. "What did you expect?"

A bright-eyed girl with a long oval face, freckles, and messy brown braids appeared among the piles of fur. She pushed back the hood of her thick, shaggy cloak.

"Don't you recognize me, Precious?" She beamed. "It's me . . . your cousin Grace."

"Oh no." Precious buried her hands deep in her lemon-yellow curls. "Not you," she wailed. "Not Cousin Grace . . ."

"How absolutely hilarious," giggled a pair of twins, Princesses Trinket and Truffle. They threw their arms around each other, squealing like two pampered, plump piglets.

"Imagine this scruffy *person* being related to Precious. It's just too funny. Are you really called Princess Grace?" they asked.

Grace nodded. She had never much liked her name. Somebody called Grace ought to be so elegant and . . . well, *graceful* . . . exactly as a princess is supposed to be.

But Princess Grace was not elegant *or* graceful. She was tall and spindly, with very big feet. Her long legs were like strands of spaghetti and—just like spaghetti—spent most of their time tangled up. She was always stumbling, tripping, and knocking things down.

Now, as Grace tried to curtsy to the headmistress, she fell flat on her bottom again, with her yak fur wound round her ankles.

"I'm sorry if I scared you all," she laughed, pushing her braids behind her ears. "I suppose it was my cloak. It's what I always wear at home. I come from the kingdom of Cragland, you see. It's cold and snowy there. But I think it may be a little too warm for it now."

"What are you doing here, Grace?" hissed Precious. "Get lost. This is *my* new school. Not yours."

"Don't be silly, Presh," said Grace, kicking the cloak away from her feet at last. "When Papa heard you were going to be a student at Tall Towers, he thought it was time I learned how to be a proper princess too. You know, all . . . princessy and royal. Just like you." Grace scratched her head. "You never know, I might even learn to curtsy properly."

"That is certainly what we are here for." Lady DuLac smiled kindly.

Some of the other princesses giggled. But Precious was scowling as if she'd sucked a slice of lemon.

"Tall Towers is the best princess school in the whole world. That's why my daddy sent me here," she spat. "But even they won't be able to help you become a proper princess. Your name might be Grace, but you are a total *dis-grace*. A royal disaster."

The twins' pink cheeks were flushed

purple with laughter. "That is *so* hilarious. You tell her, Precious."

"That's quite enough. Calm down now," said Lady DuLac.

Grace felt like turning on her big flat feet and running away. She felt like scrambling into the yak cart that had brought her here and rattling back along the rough, winding roads to the tiny, rocky kingdom of Cragland. She could reach home by dusk tomorrow night—just in time to gather round the fire in the Great Hall with Papa and his warriors. She could hear them telling the old Crag legends—stories she'd heard a hundred times—of the beasts her mighty ancestors had fought and the battles they had won. She could snuggle up with her little sister, Pip, and sip a steaming cup of yak's-milk cocoa until they fell asleep together, curled against Papa in his big wooden throne.

But if I do that, I'll never learn to be a proper princess, thought Grace. *And that's why I'm here.*

The broad smile returned to her face, and her bright hazel eyes sparkled.

"You're right, Precious. I certainly have a lot to learn," she said. "And I can't wait to get started. . . ."

CHAPTER TWO
Twelve Princesses

Now that Grace had taken off her furry cloak, the dolphins could see she wasn't a wild monster after all—just a tall, skinny girl with knobbly knees and flyaway braids. The dolphins arched their backs and swam cautiously to shore, pulling the golden school boat behind them.

"Come," said Lady DuLac, beckoning to the princesses. She stepped into the front of the beautiful shell-shaped boat, her silver

hair blowing in the breeze. "Find yourselves a seat."

"Isn't she glamorous?" whispered Grace, edging along the narrow pier and swaying dangerously as she stood on tiptoes to get a better look at the headmistress. "And aren't the dolphins amazing?" She flung her arm in the air, pointing as they rose up like six magnificent horses, ready to pull the boat to Coronet Island.

"Watch out!" snapped Precious.

"Sorry," gasped Grace, realizing she had almost hit her cousin on the nose. "Do you want to sit next to me?"

"No, I do *not*," Precious said. "I don't want you anywhere near me. I'm going to sit next to Visalotta. She's the richest princess in the whole world, and her kingdom is absolutely huge."

"Enormous," agreed the twins, who had

overheard. "Her father has three hundred and sixty-five palaces. That's one for every day of the year."

Grace could see the wealthy, dark-haired princess just ahead of them on the pier. Visalotta was wearing ruby slippers made from real jewels, and so many bangles and chains that she jingled like a bag of coins as she moved. It was hard to see her face properly because of a huge diamond tiara, so big and sparkly it was almost blinding as it flashed in the sunlight. But as a cloud plunged them into shadow for a moment, Grace thought Visalotta's big brown eyes seemed cold and sad somehow—dull against so many dazzling gems.

"Does it really matter how big your kingdom is?" Grace asked. Her own country, Cragland, was small and cold and rocky—but she loved it because it was home.

"Of course it matters!" spluttered Precious. "Just because you live somewhere smaller than a snowball . . . My mother always says her silly sister was mad to run off and marry the king of Cragland."

"But Mama and Papa were in love," said Grace. "Of course they got married." Her mother, along with Precious's mother, had been raised in a much larger, grander kingdom when they were little girls. She had left all that behind when she fell in love with Grace's father.

"She was proud to be queen of Cragland," added Grace.

She thought how sad her father had been since Mama died five years ago. It was just after baby Pip was born. Since then, Precious's family had never invited Grace or little Pip to stay with them, and they had only come to visit Cragland once. It was meant to be for a week, but they left after just one night. Her aunt and uncle said the beds were too hard, the rooms too cold, and the warriors too unruly.

"My kingdom is ten times the size of yours. Just remember that," said Precious. She pushed past Grace, almost sending her tumbling off the pier. "Hey, Visalotta!" she called. "Visalotta! Wait for me! We are going to be the very best of friends. I am sure of it."

Grace was waving her arms like a windmill, trying not to fall backward into the sea.

"Golly, Grace, you really are the most unusual princess," snorted Trinket and Truffle as they barged past. "Imagine not caring how big someone's kingdom is. Quite extraordinary."

"Oh . . . ," said Grace. She had always assumed being unusual or extraordinary was a good thing . . . but the twins didn't seem to think so.

By the time Grace reached the boat, Precious was in the front seat with Visalotta. She looked so happy to be sitting next to the rich princess that she glowed like a trophy that had just been polished. The twins Trinket and Truffle were just across the aisle, wriggling with delight. Visalotta herself looked bored. She was fiddling with her bangles and staring blankly out to sea.

Grace glanced around the boat. There were only twelve seats. And all of them were taken.

The princesses were chatting happily in pairs. Everyone except Grace had found a seat already . . . and a partner. She chewed the end of her braid. She wished she had someone to talk to.

There was only one thing to do. Grace knew Precious would be furious, but she would have to ask to share her seat.

"Scoot over," she called, hurrying toward her cousin. "I don't have anywhere else to sit."

"No. I will not *scoot over*." Precious spread out her skirts. "There are only twelve seats on this boat for a reason," she said. "There are only supposed to be twelve princesses in a class at Tall Towers Academy. You shouldn't be here. You were the last to arrive. *You* are the one too many."

Grace felt a hush fall over the boat. Every pair of eyes turned toward her.

"It would be awful to have thirteen princesses in our class," agreed Truffle.

"Everyone knows thirteen is a terribly unlucky number," said Trinket.

"Really?" Grace looked around helplessly. "I never heard that before."

"Nonsense." Lady DuLac took her hand. "That's just a silly superstition. Thirteen is no more unlucky than any other number. But it is true, we *were* on y expecting twelve princesses."

"Oh." Grace felt her stomach drop like a stone in a well. "Does that mean I can't stay and be a student at T l Towers after all?"

"There has obvio y been some sort of mix-up," said Lady DuLac kindly. "We'll look into everything when we arrive at school. We'll check your parchments and scrolls."

"Ah . . ." Grace was about to explain that she didn't have any parchments or scrolls, but Lady DuLac continued, smiling brightly.

"All we need for the moment," she said, "is somewhere for you to sit."

"Excuse me."

A quiet voice from the back of the boat made Grace turn around. It was the red-haired

princess. Grace had noticed her on the beach—
she had looked so frightened when she had
thought Grace was a monster, but had still
called out for everyone to be kind.

"I—I'm Scarlet." She blushed, her cheeks
turning pale pink, making her green eyes
shine out. "Y-you can share my seat if you
like. Only if you want to, that is . . ."

Grace had never seen anyone so pretty in
all her life. Scarlet wasn't wearing jewels or
a diamond crown, just a simple silver locket
round her neck. Her red hair tumbled down
her shoulders, and her white satin ballet
slippers were pointed on her feet as if she
might dance away across the boat at any
moment. She seemed so elegant, so *princessy*.
Yes, that was the only word for it.

"I'd love to sit with you!" Grace beamed.
She bounded down the aisle, making the
boat rock from side to side.

"Don't fall overboard!" cried Scarlet as Grace reached the seat, almost tumbling on top of her.

"It would be just my luck if I did!" Grace laughed.

Scarlet's face broke into a huge smile. "I was nervous about the journey to the island," she said. "I'm a terrible worrier. But with two people between me and the side of the boat, I feel so much more snug and safe."

She turned to a tiny, delicate-looking princess with ebony hair perched on the other seat. "Is it all right if Grace sits next to us, Izumi?" she asked. "You're not too squashed, are you? Do you still have room to sketch?"

"It's fine." Princess Izumi looked up for a moment from a picture she was drawing in a little gold-edged book.

"Thank you," said Grace, but Izumi had already turned away. She was frowning in concentration, chewing her pencil and sketching again.

"Everyone comfortable?" said Lady DuLac. "Then off we go." She blew three short blasts on a silver whistle.

The dolphins dived forward, and the boat set sail across the sparkling Sapphire Sea.

"Next stop, Tall Towers Academy," said Lady DuLac.

The princesses clapped politely.

"Yippee!" Grace threw her arms in the air and cheered. "My mother was a student at Tall Towers. She used to tell me such wonderful stories about it," she said, holding Scarlet's trembling hand as they sped across the waves. "Think of all the adventures we'll have. Just so long as they let me stay . . ."

CHAPTER THREE
Tall Towers

If the ride in a boat pulled by dolphins was exciting for the new princesses, arriving at Coronet Island for the first time was even more thrilling.

Grace couldn't help leaping to her feet as the island came into view at last. Jutting up like a crown in the middle of the Sapphire Sea, it was dotted with golden sandy beaches, emerald-green meadows, jade woods, and diamond lakes sparkling like jewels. Far away, to the north, rose pearl-topped mountains sprinkled with snow.

But best of all, built high on the cliffs above the horseshoe harbor, was Tall Towers Princess Academy, with its marble walls, cool courtyards, and twisting towers spiraling high into the cloudless blue sky.

"Wow," said Grace. "Wowee!"

"It's beautiful," breathed Scarlet.

"It's perfect," said Izumi, speaking for only the second time since they had left the mainland. "Like someone designed it from a dream." She was sketching like crazy, her hand darting backward and forward across the page.

"Please make your way up the cobble path and into the main courtyard," said Lady DuLac. "Don't worry. It is just you First Years here at the moment. The princesses in all the other classes will arrive when the term starts officially tomorrow."

I wonder if I will still be here by then, thought Grace. She couldn't bear the thought of being sent home—not now that she had seen Tall Towers for herself. It was like an enchanted fairy-tale palace.

"Come on." Grace linked arms with Scarlet. She was a little scared of Izumi, who seemed so serious as she concentrated on her drawing, but Grace held out her arm for her too as Izumi put her sketchbook away. "If you two are looking after me, I can't trip over my big feet and fall flat on my nose," she said.

Izumi smiled.

The princesses all chatted happily—gasping and pointing, calling out to each other as they hurried up the winding path through rose gardens, under archways of honeysuckle, and past graceful statues and tinkling fountains.

Even Precious was smiling, and the twins helped Grace to her feet when she tripped over a little stone birdbath.

But the minute the girls turned in to the grand marble courtyard, the chat and laughter suddenly stopped. Poof—it was as if a candle had been snuffed out.

A stern gray woman was standing in front

of them, straight as a pillar, glaring at them and barking out their names, which she ticked off a list with a black feather quill.

"Do you think she's a witch?" mouthed Grace.

Scarlet made a noise like a frightened foal.

"No. I am not a witch," said the woman, who certainly seemed to have magical powers for hearing even the tiniest whisper. "I am Fairy Godmother Flint, and I do not expect such rudeness from a young princess."

"I'm so sorry," said Grace, standing as straight as she could. The fairy godmother looked her up and down as if she was a tall weed in a field of flowers. "I didn't mean to be rude. I—"

"Silence." The fairy godmother held up a thin, bent finger. "I am your First Year teacher."

Grace remembered her mother saying once that all the teachers at Tall Towers Academy were fairy godmothers. In the storybooks Grace had at home, fairy godmothers were always soft, plump people with shining eyes and rosy cheeks. Fairy Godmother Flint was nothing like that. She was whip-thin, with a chin as sharp as a pencil and eyes the color of stone.

"What is your name?" asked the fairy godmother, running the scratchy tip of her quill down her list.

"I'm Princess Grace. . . ."

"Hmm."

There was a silence, which seemed to Grace to last a thousand heartbeats.

"I have no Princess Grace on my list," said Fairy Godmother Flint at last. "Let me see your parchments and scrolls."

"Oh . . . erm . . ." Grace held out her empty hands. "I don't have any parchments . . . or any scrolls."

"Nothing?" Fairy Godmother Flint raised

one thin eyebrow like the wing of a bat. "That is most irregular. No scroll of acceptance to the school? No parchment of registration? No completed uniform list?"

"No." Grace smiled helplessly. "I didn't know I would need anything like that. My father heard Precious was coming. She's my cousin, you see . . . and he . . . he just sort of thought it would be all right if I showed up too. We hoped . . . because I am a princess and everything . . . that might be how it worked."

"That is *not* how it works," said the fairy godmother. "I have only twelve names on my list. There are only ever twelve princesses in a class at Tall Towers Academy. That is the tradition. *Your* name is not on my list. *You* are number thirteen. *You* must go home."

Precious was almost dancing with delight.

"Told you. I said you weren't supposed to be here."

"Home?" The word stuck in Grace's throat. She hadn't even made it out of the courtyard and into the main school.

"Wait." Grace spun around, desperately searching for Lady DuLac.

"Please, Headmistress," she called, spotting her standing a little way off beneath the shade of an old peach tree. "Don't make me leave. Isn't there anything you can do?"

"It seems very simple," said Lady DuLac. She reached up and picked a glistening golden fruit from the branch above her. "We will let the unicorns decide."

The headmistress stepped forward and addressed the princesses. "As you probably know, every girl who attends Tall Towers receives a unicorn on her first day at the school. These creatures will be your loyal companions—you will ride them, groom them, and care for them every day that you are here."

A murmur of excitement ran around the courtyard.

"I demand one with an emerald horn!" cried Precious. "My daddy says I can take whichever one I like."

"We want matching ones. With golden hooves," roared the twins.

"Ah," said Lady DuLac, never raising her voice. "That is the point. A princess does not get to choose her own unicorn. They choose you. These magical beasts come out of the Jade Forest, bringing all the wisdom and knowledge they have drunk from the mountain streams."

Grace's heart pounded. More than

anything else, she had been dreaming of getting her own unicorn when she came to Tall Towers.

"If no unicorn comes forward for you, then you must return home," said Lady DuLac, touching Grace gently on the shoulder. "Do you understand that?"

Grace nodded. "Yes," she whispered. Her voice caught in her throat. "I understand."

Everything would be decided by the unicorns.

CHAPTER FOUR
Unicorns

Grace jiggled from foot to foot.

She had longed to meet a real unicorn all her life. Now it mattered more than ever. If no unicorn came for her, she would have to leave the school, and her dream of learning to be a real princess would be shattered.

"Do you think they'll bite?" Scarlet gulped as the princesses gathered under the big shady tree in the courtyard.

"No. Unicorns don't eat princesses. Just peaches." Grace smiled.

"Welcome, my dears." A plump, happy-looking man with a long ginger-colored mustache had appeared beneath the tree. "I am Sir Rolling-Trot, the school riding coach," he said, bowing with a flourish. "Come and pick a fruit. We're going to make our way to Silver Meadow. When we get there, each princess must hold out a peach. The unicorn that chooses you will step out of the forest and eat from your hand."

Here goes nothing, thought Grace. She stretched up and picked the biggest, ripest peach she could reach.

But the squishy fruit was so ripe, juice squirted everywhere.

"Whoops!" cried Grace.

Scarlet jumped sideways like an elegant ballet dancer, just in time to avoid getting sprayed with juice.

But Precious was not so quick. A sticky

yellow spurt hit her right in the eye. "Look out!" she wailed. Her dress was spattered with juice. "I'll get you back for this, Grace."

"Sorry," Grace mumbled. "I just thought a nice ripe fruit would be best."

"It doesn't matter which peach you have," spat Precious. "No unicorn is ever going to pick you, Grace. You don't belong at Tall Towers."

"We'll just have to wait and see, won't we?" said Grace. But for a moment, her eyes tingled on the edge of tears as she hoped that Precious was wrong. She looked down at the soggy fruit in her hand. Sweet, sticky juice dripped between her fingers and splashed onto her shoes.

"Ready, my dears?" said Sir Rolling-Trot. "Follow me." He raised his sword and lunged forward as if he was leading a charge of knights on horseback.

Scarlet hung back for a moment, her face as white as a scroll.

"Come on," said Grace, wiping her sticky fingers on her skirt and grabbing Scarlet's hand. "We'll do this together."

They followed the other princesses out of the courtyard and through the grounds toward Silver Meadow.

"Shhh!" said Sir Rolling-Trot as they reached the edge of a paddock dotted with wildflowers. "This is where the unicorns will come."

"Look," whispered Izumi. She was staring into a haze of mist where the meadow joined the dark Jade Forest. "I can see one already. It's as white as moonlight."

The unicorn's horn glinted in the pale sun.

Grace gasped. She had never seen anything so beautiful in all her life. "Come on!" she urged, holding out her peach along with the other princesses. "Come to me, beauty."

But the little creature trotted straight across the grass and nibbled the small, firm fruit from Izumi's hand.

"Good show!" cried Sir Rolling-Trot, holding out a length of silver rope for Izumi to tie around the unicorn's neck. "Look after him well, Princess. From now on, he will always be yours."

"Thank you, sir." Izumi curtsied. Then she smiled at Grace. "Do you mind if I call him Beauty? Like you said when you held out your peach just now."

"Of course not." Grace dearly wished this first unicorn had chosen her. She would know then that she belonged at Tall Towers for sure. But she couldn't help smiling at Izumi. "Beauty is the perfect name for him," she said. He suited the artistic princess so well.

Six more unicorns had come out of the forest now, and Grace held out her soggy peach, wishing one of them would come toward her. Not all of them were white; some were gray or dappled. A golden palomino made its way straight to Precious.

"I shall call him Champion," she crowed, snatching the rope from Sir Rolling-Trot and flinging it around the unicorn's neck.

"I'm going to paint his hooves silver and tie his mane and tail with ribbons."

"Good idea." The twins clapped with delight. They already had two fat, pink strawberry roan unicorns that they'd christened Cherry Puff and Berry Pie.

Precious led her golden unicorn away. She was pulling on the rope and jabbing at him to hold his head high. "Stand straight, you stupid animal," she snapped.

Poor Champion, thought Grace.

Just then a pale, shimmering unicorn that glistened like diamonds trotted forward and took the peach from Visalotta's ringed fingers.

"Ooooh. You should call him Sparkles," cooed the twins.

"Maybe." Visalotta shrugged. Even the magnificent unicorn didn't make her smile.

Precious, meanwhile, looked like she was

going to faint with envy as her rich friend slid a rope around the creature's shiny neck.

"I wish this was all over." Scarlet shivered, squeezing Grace's hand. "We're the last two to be picked."

She was right. They were the only princesses still without a unicorn. Grace wanted to run into the forest and search among the trees. She would climb the mountains if she had to. Anything to find a unicorn of her own.

But Scarlet was holding her tight. "Don't let go of me," she begged.

A pretty, dappled gray unicorn had come to the edge of the forest. Grace squeezed Scarlett's hand.

"Look," gasped Grace. "I bet this one's yours—he looks so friendly."

"*She,*" corrected Sir Rolling-Trot. "That unicorn is a girl."

The little mare trotted closer.

Scarlet lowered her peach.

"You take her, Grace," she said. "There don't seem to be any more, and you *must* get a unicorn or you'll be sent away from the school."

Grace shook her head. "This one is for you. I'm sure of it."

There was no doubt. The pretty little unicorn was just right for Scarlet. She trotted quietly forward and gently bowed her head so that the trembling princess could stroke her ears.

"She's so soft," whispered Scarlet. "I'll call her Velvet." She turned and smiled at Grace. "You were right. There was nothing to be scared of at all."

But Grace barely heard her. She was staring hard at the forest.

The mist had cleared, and the meadow was empty.

"Strange," said Sir Rolling-Trot, twirling his ginger-colored mustache and striding up and down. "I've never had a princess without a unicorn before."

"It's because Grace is extra," said Precious. "She's number thirteen. She's not supposed to be here."

"Numbers don't matter," said Sir Rolling-Trot. "If you deserve a unicorn, one will come."

Grace held her peach straight in front of her. Her hands were shaking. "Come on," she coaxed, staring at the empty meadow and the trees beyond. "Come on, my unicorn. I know you're there."

Sir Rolling-Trot looked down at the soggy mess in her hand.

"Tut, tut," he muttered. "Is that the best you could do? The animal chooses the princess, remember. It has to *want* to belong to you, or it will never come."

Grace heard Precious snicker. But she didn't turn. She stared hard at the forest.

"Come on, my unicorn. Come on."

The other princesses were leading their animals away now. Only Scarlet and Izumi were still waiting for her. But Beauty was getting restless, pawing at the ground. Even gentle Velvet was swishing her tail.

Sir Rolling-Trot cleared his throat. "Time to head back to school, I'm afraid," he said. "There'll be no more unicorns today."

"Please," begged Grace. "Just a little longer." She would stay here all night if she had to.

But then a branch moved.

The leaves rustled.

Now the trees were shaking as if a wild boar was charging through them.

Crash!

A shaggy black-and-white unicorn burst out of the forest. He was covered in twigs and leaves.

"What is *that* thing?" laughed Precious as the princesses turned back to see what was making such a noise. "It looks like it's come through a bush backward."

But Grace felt her heart leap with joy.

The hairy unicorn thundered across the meadow, heading straight toward her.

"My unicorn," she breathed.

"Good gracious. A rough coat. How unusual," said Sir Rolling-Trot. "I haven't seen one of those for thirty years."

The unicorn's long black-and-white mane flowed almost to the grass.

"What a freak," Precious said. "He looks like a giant, hairy billy goat with only one horn."

Grace felt butterflies somersault in her

stomach as the shaggy unicorn skidded to
a stop and slurped the squishy peach from
her fingers.

"Hello, there." She smiled.

The unicorn butted her with his muzzle,
and she toppled over backward onto the grass.

"He even behaves like a billy goat," snorted Precious.

"Then that's what I'll call him." Grace smiled. "Billy. It's the perfect name."

She looked up into the unicorn's dark, trusting eyes. And he peered down at her from under his flowing mane.

"I don't care if he does look like a goat— or even a hairy yak," said Grace. "Maybe he's not as smooth as gold or as shiny as diamonds. But I love him. He chose me, and he's mine."

As if to agree, Billy took hold of the end of one of Grace's braids in his teeth and tugged at it.

"Thank you," she whispered, rubbing his soft shaggy ears. "Now I can stay at Tall Towers and learn to be a proper princess. Just you wait, Billy. . . . We're going to make the perfect team."

CHAPTER FIVE
The Dormitory

The princesses settled the unicorns into their new stables, each with a bundle of fresh hay and slices of fresh peach.

Billy tipped over the first three buckets of water that Grace filled for him from the well.

"You're just as clumsy as I am," she laughed, sloshing a fourth bucket over the floor by mistake.

"Tomorrow you will learn to groom your unicorns, and eventually you will ride them," said Sir Rolling-Trot. "But for now you'd

better go with Old Flintheart . . . I mean Fairy Godmother Flint. She doesn't like to be kept waiting, you know."

Grace giggled as he pointed to the gray figure of the fairy godmother standing at the edge of the yard like a watchful hawk. Flintheart was the perfect nickname for her.

"Come along, Young Majesties. It is time to find out where you are sleeping," she said.

"How exciting!" cried Grace.

Now that she knew she could stay at Tall Towers, she leapt forward to be the first in line.

Splat!

She felt something squelch under her foot.

Fairy Godmother Flint raised a bony finger. "Please wipe that off before returning to school," she sniffed, pointing at something nasty on the bottom of Grace's shoe.

"Typical. It's not very princessy to tread

in unicorn poo," sneered Precious.

"Not very princessy at all," sighed the fairy godmother.

"I suppose I should look where I'm going in a stable yard." Grace smiled, holding her nose. She hurried to the meadow and wiped her shoes in the long grass. Then she charged back across the courtyard to catch up with the rest of the group.

By the time she reached them, they were gathered in a long hallway just inside the main doors. The walls were covered with notice boards, declarations, and scrolls.

The girls were crowded around a list of names.

Grace squeezed through and read the scroll for herself.

She read the list twice to make sure. But her name was definitely not there.

I've been left out again, she thought.

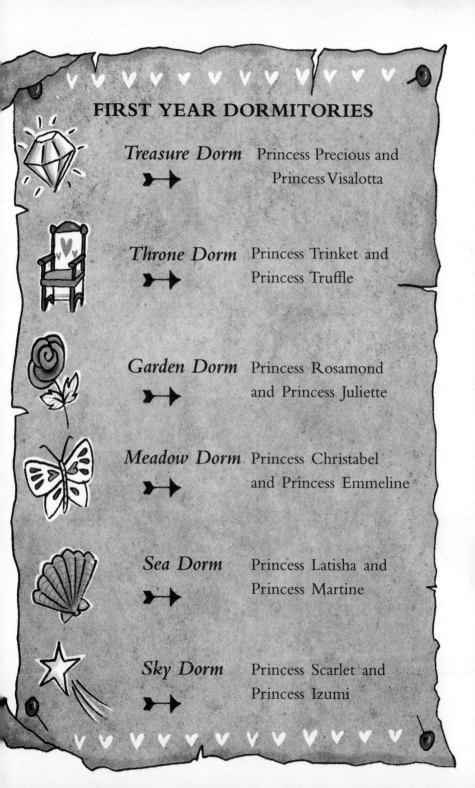

FIRST YEAR DORMITORIES

Treasure Dorm ➤ Princess Precious and Princess Visalotta

Throne Dorm ➤ Princess Trinket and Princess Truffle

Garden Dorm ➤ Princess Rosamond and Princess Juliette

Meadow Dorm ➤ Princess Christabel and Princess Emmeline

Sea Dorm ➤ Princess Latisha and Princess Martine

Sky Dorm ➤ Princess Scarlet and Princess Izumi

"Poor you!" gasped Scarlet. "I'm sure they'll find you somewhere just as soon as they can."

"Looks like you'll have to sleep in a barn." Precious giggled nastily.

"That's a wonderful idea!" Grace jumped up and down with excitement. "Don't worry about me not having a dormitory, Fairy Godmother," she called out. "I can sleep in the stables with Billy."

"No," said Old Flintheart. She reached to pick a clump of hay out of Grace's hair. "Princesses do *not* sleep in the stables. Ever."

"Grace can't share with me, Fairy Godmother. Even if she is my cousin," said Precious, looking worried. "There wouldn't be room. Visalotta will need an extra wardrobe for all her clothes as it is."

"And Grace wouldn't want to share with us," said Princess Trinket. "Truffle snores."

"No, I do not. That's a lie." Truffle blushed like a furious tomato.

"Yes, you do." Trinket kicked her sister. "You snore *really* badly, Truffle. Remember?"

"Oh," said Truffle, suddenly understanding. "She's right, Fairy Godmother. Grace certainly wouldn't want to share with us. I do snore. Like a trumpet. We both do."

"Like two trumpets," squealed Trinket, and the twins collapsed in snorts of laughter.

"I don't mind where I go," said Grace. It wasn't true, though. She had dearly hoped that she could be with Scarlet. But the red-haired princess had moved away from the notice board. She had her arm round Izumi, and they were whispering together as if they had a secret to share.

Probably planning a midnight feast for their first night in the new dorm, thought Grace sadly.

She glanced back at the list. Scarlet and

Izumi's room was called Sky Dorm. It sounded so exciting, as if it was hidden away in the clouds.

"I suppose we could clear a bed for you in the sickroom," sighed Fairy Godmother Flint. "But I don't know what we'll do if somebody comes down with the measles."

"The sickroom? Oh, poor Grace." Scarlet rushed forward and grabbed her hand. "It would be so lonely. And you'd aways feel as if you were ill."

"You're welcome to share with us if you'd like to," said Izumi, taking Grace's other hand. "We were just talking about it."

"Please say you will," begged Scarlet. "It might be a bit of a squeeze, but it would be so much fun. I'd hate to think of you in the sickroom all alone."

A smile spread across Grace's face. "Whoopee!" she cried. Her voice echoed through the marble corridors like a clanging bell. "Whoopee! Whoopee!"

Grace flung her arms around her two friends' shoulders and kicked her long, skinny legs high in the air. "I can't think of anything that I would like more than to share a dormitory with you." She grinned.

"Dignity, please." Fairy Godmother Flint scowled.

But even Old Flintheart's stern expression couldn't stop Grace from tapping her feet and whistling as she climbed the narrow stairs up to Sky Dorm.

On the way past, she peered in at Treasure Dorm, which looked out onto the big gray vaults where all the school's gold was stored. Precious was delighted with the room because it had a diamond door handle and golden bedsheets made of shiny silk.

The twins were just as pleased with Throne

Dorm, which overlooked the ceremonial hall, where important meetings with royal visitors were held. Grace peeked round the door and blinked. The bright purple bedspreads and vivid red velvet walls made her eyes water.

But Garden Dorm, Meadow Dorm, and Sea Dorm were all lovely, with pretty decorations of flowers, butterflies, or seashells on the wallpaper.

"You're so lucky," Grace told the other princesses when she saw their views of the lawns, the fields, or the horseshoe-shaped harbor.

"Sky Dorm is farther up," said Fairy Godmother Flint. "It's right in the attic."

"All the more stairs to fall down," laughed Precious, poking her head out of her door as Grace clomped on, up the narrow, twisting steps.

At last, Izumi, Scarlet, and Grace reached

the very top of Dormitory Tower. They saw a little white door tucked away in the rooftop.

"Ready?" The three new friends put their hands on the old brass doorknob. "Push," said Grace.

The door swung open, and the girls fell into the middle of a little round room.

"It's like an artist's studio," gasped Izumi as light flooded down on them.

"And it's perfect for dancing," said Scarlet. She spun across the wooden floor in a graceful pirouette.

Grace, for once, could not speak at all.

The pretty white dormitory seemed the loveliest of them all. It had glass skylights in the roof and a view of the whole of Coronet Island.

There were two little white beds already and plenty of room for a third tucked in between them.

"It's the sort of place where princess dreams come true," said Grace at last. She tried to spin like Scarlet had done, but landed with a thump on her bottom.

"Oops!" She grinned. "My dreams *will* come true. I just have to practice a little first."

Later that night, as the stars shone down through the skylight, the three girls prepared for a midnight feast.

"I hope we don't get caught," whispered Scarlet, passing around a box of delicate white cookies wrapped in pink tissue paper. "Old Flintheart scares the life out of me."

"We'll just have to keep our voices down," mouthed Izumi. She gently popped the cork on a bottle of fizzy lemonade.

"I was so hoping we'd have a feast," said Grace, offering around a handkerchief filled with yak's-milk fudge. "It only got a *little*

bit fluffy in the pocket of my cloak."

"Yikes. It looks like furry caterpillars," squealed Scarlet, peeping under the corner of the handkerchief.

"Or dragon droppings!" cried Grace, grabbing the biggest piece of fudge and chasing the others around the room with it.

The girls laughed so loud, it was surprising that Fairy Godmother Flint didn't hear them from her office at the bottom of Dormitory Tower and come thundering up the stairs.

"Oh, Grace, we are never going to be bored with you here." Scarlet giggled as the three of them collapsed in a heap on the floor. Tears of laughter streamed helplessly down their cheeks.

"Now for a pillow fight," said Grace.

CHAPTER SIX
The Uniform List

Thud!

During the night, Grace rolled out of bed.

She was so used to doing this at home that she didn't even wake up.

But in the morning, Scarlet and Izumi found her sleeping in a heap on the dormitory floor.

"Wake up," they whispered. "It's nearly breakfast time."

Grace blinked. From where she was lying, she could see straight into a full-length mirror.

Her hair was caught in the springs of the bed above her head—it had probably been like that for most of the night. As she untangled herself, she saw that it was now sticking up in crazy clumps, like an angry chicken's feathers.

"Ow!" She winced, pulling a last tangle free from the bedsprings and scrambling to her feet.

Izumi and Scarlet were already dressed neatly in the pretty white pinafores with blue sashes that all the Tall Towers princesses were supposed to wear.

"We'll help you get ready," said Izumi.

"But I don't have a pinafore," sighed Grace. As she hadn't received all the proper scrolls and lists, she didn't have any of the right clothes with her.

"Where am I supposed to find these things? And how much will it all cost?" she groaned, staring at the regulation uniform list that had been left on the end of her bed. "I know Papa is a king. But I don't think he is a very rich one."

She ran her finger down the long scroll: "*Indoor shoes, outdoor shoes, riding jacket, riding hat, riding boots, ballet leotard, ballet tutu, ballet cardigan, ballet shoes, ballroom dress, ballroom shoes, handkerchiefs (white—12), gloves (leather), gloves (wool), gloves (lace), parasol . . .*"

"I have a spare pinafore you can borrow," said Izumi as she began to braid one side of Grace's hair and Scarlet started on the other. "I can let down the hem."

But they knew it was hopeless. Izumi was so tiny—like a little china doll beside Grace.

"Your pinafore would be more like a bib than a dress on me. I'd end up showing my knickers," laughed Grace. She glanced down at the scroll again. "And it says here they are supposed to be the regulation school kind—white . . . and frilly . . . My knickers are bright blue with red spots."

"Stop it!" squealed Scarlet, who was a big giggler. She let go of Grace's braid, and it unraveled in her hands. "You'll make me wet *my* knickers if I laugh this much."

"I bet yours *are* regulation white and frilly, though," spluttered Grace.

"I beg your pardon?" Fairy Godmother Flint appeared in the doorway. "A princess never discusses her underwear."

"Sorry. It's just I don't seem to have quite the right things," said Grace. She scrambled into the same creased clothes she had worn the day before. She caught sight of herself in the mirror again and tried not to giggle. One side of her hair was braided, and Izumi had tied a ribbon around it in a beautiful double bow—but the other side was still as wild as a bunch of hay.

"Tut, tut." The First Year teacher scowled down her thin nose. "This will not do, Young Majesty."

She sent Scarlet and Izumi off to breakfast in the Dining Tower and ordered Grace to see the seamstress, Fairy Godmother Pom.

When she reached the Sewing Tower, Grace pulled on the long red tassel that rang the tingling gold doorbell.

"Come in, come in!" Fairy Godmother Pom beamed. She looked exactly like a fairy godmother is supposed to look, round and plump and smiling—as different from Fairy Godmother Flint as a ball of knitting wool is from an iron nail.

"How lovely to meet you, young Gracie," she said, chattering as she led the way through a maze of sewing machines and tailor's dummies. There were jars overflowing

with buttons and pins, rolls of bright material and reels of thread.

"I remember Princess Dawn, your dear mother," chortled Fairy Godmother Pom. "Before she married your father and became Queen Dawn, that is. I had to let down the hem of her Tall Towers pinafore three times in her first term. I even made her wedding dress for her. Did she ever tell you that?"

"No . . . I don't think so." Grace stumbled over the end of a roll of green velvet and steadied herself against a table for a moment. She knew so little about her mother, really. It was strange to think she had been looked after by this kind, happy woman. Strange to think she had been a new girl on her first day at Tall Towers, just like Grace was now.

"Forgive me. I'm a silly old chatterbox," said Fairy Godmother Pom. She spun around like a bobbin of bright thread and gathered Grace into a warm hug. "You had so little time with your mother. You were so young when she passed away, and your poor sister, Princess Pip, just a baby . . . and here's me, chattering on about all my memories. I didn't want to upset you."

"I like it when people talk about her," said Grace. "Papa never even mentions her name. He says it makes him too sad. And when Pip asks me questions about Mama, I often have to make things up because I don't know the real answers for sure. But you *remember* her—you *knew* her. Ever since she was a schoolgirl."

"Anytime you want, you just ask me about her. I shouldn't say this, but she was a bit of a favorite with me," said Fairy Godmother Pom. She took Grace's hand and led her toward a huge wooden wardrobe. "She was so kind and polite. And funny too. Not like her sister, Princess Greya, your aunt. Queen Greya, as she is now."

"Precious's mum." Grace nodded.

"Could sour milk in a churn, that one," sighed Fairy Godmother Pom. "She was horrid to your mother. Just because Dawn was her baby sister. Three years younger and twice as smart."

The little fairy godmother stood on tiptoes and heaved open the doors of the huge wardrobe.

"Now we'd better get you set up with some clothes," she said. "Otherwise old Flintheart . . . I mean, Fairy Godmother Flint . . . will string me up with the laundry."

"Wow!" Grace's mouth dropped open like a drawbridge. The wardrobe was stuffed full of dresses and skirts, hats and shoes, parasols and petticoats in every color of the rainbow.

"Where did all these things come from?" she gasped.

"Lost-and-found—years of the stuff," said Fairy Godmother Pom. "Now you give me that uniform scroll. We'll find you everything you need here. There's even a diamond tiara stuffed away somewhere."

Fairy Godmother Pom's front end disappeared into the wardrobe like a bear going into a cave.

"One ballet tutu. That should fit you!" she cried, tossing a white net skirt out from behind the hanging rail. It landed in a large empty trunk by Grace's feet. "And a cardigan too. Riding jacket—dark blue. It's lovely material, that one." A thick navy coat flew out of the wardrobe door. "Riding gloves. Lace fan . . ."

In no time at all, the trunk was nearly full.

"Shoes might be a bit of a problem," said Fairy Godmother Pom, shuffling backward out of the wardrobe and looking down at Grace's very large feet. "You'll just have to make do with what you have for now." She pointed to the big, brown lace-up walking boots Grace was wearing. "Meanwhile, I'll send a message to the village. The cobbler will come and fit you for indoor shoes, outdoor shoes, ballet slippers, and everything else you need."

"Really?" gasped Grace. "All those shoes just for me?" She had only ever owned walking boots and a pair of comfy yak-skin slippers before now.

Fairy Godmother Pom nodded. "Only the pinafore left and you'll look like a proper Tall Towers princess."

She selected the longest white dress from a row of pinafores.

"Go on, then, Gracie. Pop behind the curtain and slip that on," she said.

"Well, I never. Don't you look elegant!" Fairy Godmother Pom smiled when Grace came out of the cubicle.

She reached up to braid the second side of Grace's hair. Then she wound a bright blue sash around Grace's waist and tied it in a bow.

"Perfect," she said, leading Grace toward a tall mirror in the corner.

"Oh." Grace half curtsied—confused for a moment, thinking some other princess must have come into the room.

"That's you, you silly duckling," chuckled Fairy Godmother Pom.

Grace stood and stared. She had never in all her life believed she could look like this. Her dress was so perfect and white.

"I look like a real princess," she whispered.

"Yes, you do," agreed Fairy Godmother Pom. "The real thing. Without a doubt."

CHAPTER SEVEN
Deportment

The uniform fitting took so long that Grace had missed breakfast in the Dining Tower. But Fairy Godmother Pom insisted on making her a drink and toasting some crumpets on the fire.

By the time Grace hurried across the courtyard to the First Year Common Room, her perfect white pinafore already had a sprinkle of crumbs, a drizzle of honey, and a splash of hot chocolate down the front.

Izumi and Scarlet thought she looked perfect, though.

"But it's secondhand," sniffed Precious. "From the lost-and-found."

"Sometimes old outfits can be even better than new ones," said Izumi, who loved to design and make her own clothes. "You're so lucky to have explored the Sewing Tower already, Grace. I've heard Fairy Godmother Pom has some amazing vintage ball gowns up there. Some of them are over a hundred years old . . . and there are capes and gloves and parasols as well."

"It was wonderful," agreed Grace. "I've never seen so many beautiful dresses in all my life."

She didn't care what Precious said. She loved how light and floaty her pinafore felt. She couldn't resist spinning in a circle, just to watch the skirt spread out around her with the blue ribbons from the sash streaming behind.

"Don't forget you still don't have regulation knickers on." Scarlet giggled as Grace's skirt flew up around her ears.

"Come on. We'd better hurry," said a sporty princess named Latisha, sprinting out the door. "We have a deportment lesson with old Flintheart first thing."

"Deportment?" said Grace, tugging her skirt toward her knees. "What's that?"

"You'll find out," laughed Precious. "Basically it's your worst nightmare, Grace."

For once, Grace had to agree with Precious. Deportment did turn out to be her worst nightmare.

The class took place in the beautiful glass ballet studio beside the lake. First,

Fairy Godmother Flint stood the girls in a line.

"Deportment is all about posture," she said, handing them each a leather-bound book. "A princess must learn how to stand straight. How to hold her head steady. And how *not* to fall over her own big feet."

This last comment seemed to be aimed directly at Grace.

"Find a space and hold your book out in front of you," said Flintheart.

Thank goodness for that, thought Grace. *Whatever deportment is, we are only going to read about it for today.* That didn't sound too bad. Grace glanced down at the thick red spine of her book.

Princess Manners for Beginners by B. Royal.

"Now place the books on your heads," said Flintheart sternly.

"On our *heads*?" Grace laughed out loud.

She was sure she must have heard wrong. But the other girls were already gliding around the room in time to Fairy Godmother Flint's fast clap, their shoulders back and their books balanced perfectly on top of their heads.

"Excellent, excellent," said Flintheart.

Bam!

Grace had taken only one step when *Princess Manners for Beginners* crashed to the floor.

"Honestly, Princess Grace," sighed Fairy Godmother Flint. "Have you never had a deportment lesson before? Didn't your governess teach you the basics at least?"

"Er—I didn't have a governess," said Grace.

"No governess?" Flintheart sounded amazed.

She would have been less surprised if I said I had grown a bright green beard, thought Grace.

"Who taught you your lessons?" asked Flintheart, her eyes wide in disbelief.

"Everybody, really." Grace shrugged. "Gogo, the wise hermit, taught me how to read and write. Haggle, the head herdsman, taught me how to milk a yak."

The princesses laughed.

"Yuck," said Precious.

"Jape, my father's jester, tried to teach me how to juggle with cheese." Grace smiled. "But I was hopeless at that. He did tell me some really funny jokes, though. There's this one about a yak who is halfway up a mountain. The only trouble is, he is bursting to go for a wee, so—"

"Stop! Enough!" cried Fairy Godmother Flint. "A princess *never* tells toilet jokes."

The class giggled.

"It's not rude," said Grace. "Not really . . ." But something about old Flintheart's ash-gray face told Grace that the teacher's idea of what was rude might be very different from Jape the jester's.

Flintheart clapped her hands. "Princesses, please continue to walk around the room. Meanwhile, Princess Grace, you can practice staying silent and standing still."

She led Grace to the side of the studio.

"Stand straight with your back against a pillar," she said, placing *Princess Manners for Beginners* on top of Grace's head again. "If you do not move, the book will not fall off. This is a basic lesson in deportment that most princesses learn while they are still toddlers."

Grace smiled, trying to imagine her little sister, Pip, standing still with a book on her head.

Flintheart shook her head in despair. "There is no need to grin like a jester. High spirits have never helped a book stay on anybody's head."

Grace relaxed her face and stretched her neck. If standing with a book on her head really would make her a better princess, she would give it her very best shot.

But she found it almost impossible to stand still. She could see the older princesses outside the window, hurrying to their classes now that the Tall Towers term had begun for real. They all looked so sparkly and poised—like swans gliding past in their white frocks.

Two girls who must have been Sixth Years seemed to shimmer as they floated across the lake in a silver rowing boat. Their heads were held high and their backs as straight as rulers.

I suppose deportment lessons taught them to sit like that, thought Grace, lifting her shoulders.

Bam!

Princess Manners for Beginners crashed to the floor.

"That is the end of the class," sighed Flintheart, picking up the heavy book and handing it back to Grace. "I suggest you practice in your own time, Young Majesty."

"I will. I promise," said Grace.

"Next lesson I shall have a look at your

curtsies," said Flintheart as the class filed out of the room.

"Oh no. Not curtsies," said Grace when they were all on the grass outside. "You know how bad I am at those."

"Just try to feel elegant," said a graceful princess named Christabel. She dipped her knees and bobbed low.

Grace tried to copy.

Her bottom stuck out behind her like a long-legged ostrich about to lay an egg.

"Hilarious," snorted the twins. "But certainly *not* elegant."

"Practice makes perfect." Grace shrugged, colliding with them both as she swung her bottom round the other way.

CHAPTER EIGHT
New Challenges

The next morning, the First Years filed into the Grand Ballroom for an assembly with the rest of the school. It turned out that being able to do a perfect curtsy was going to be much more important than Grace could ever have guessed.

"I have exciting news," announced Lady DuLac. "Tall Towers is to host a Grand Winter Tournament at the end of the term. Brave knights will arrive with their magnificent

horses. They will dress in suits of armor and joust in the Silver Meadow."

A murmur of excitement buzzed through the Grand Ballroom.

"My cousin Wilbur is a knight," whispered Scarlet. "Although he is not a very brave one."

"I think knights are magnificent," swooned a pretty Fifth Year with blond curls piled as high as a chimney.

"And *so* handsome," giggled her friend.

"The school will be on show," continued Lady DuLac, her voice rising gently above the chatter. "As the tournament will be on the last day of the term, your parents are invited to come and watch. There will be kings and queens from every kingdom. Each class will have a different task to perform to make sure that we at Tall Towers are the perfect host. I know each and every one of you will make me proud."

Grace felt she would do *anything* to make the beautiful headmistress proud.

"The First Years will begin the event with a parade." Lady DuLac smiled. "You will carry flags and curtsy to the visiting kings and queens. Second Years will sing to the audience before the jousting starts. Third Years will . . ."

Grace didn't hear what the next classes would be doing. Her head was spinning. The First Years would have to curtsy . . . in front of a crowd of royal visitors.

Beside her, Izumi was sketching a row of curtsying princesses in her little gold book.

Grace turned the other way and tugged at Scarlet's sleeve. "I thought curtsying for Flintheart was going to be bad enough," she hissed.

"I know. Imagine being in front of all those important people." Scarlet trembled.

"Shhh!" warned Fairy Godmother Flint.

"The Fifth Years will be in charge of festive decorations," Lady DuLac was saying.

"Decorations? We'll never get to meet the knights if we're stuck up a pillar fiddling with a bunch of prickly holly," Grace heard the girl with chimney hair complain.

Grace wished she was in the Fifth Year already—fixing prickly holly to a wall sounded far better than curtsying.

"And the Sixth Years will ride their unicorns in a galloping display," concluded the headmistress.

Now that is something I really would love to do, thought Grace.

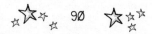

Every opportunity she could find in those first few weeks at school, Grace slipped away to the stables to spend time with Billy.

The big, playful unicorn was just as loving and kind as she had thought he would be, although he did have a very naughty habit of nibbling her braids as if they were made from hay.

Grace had to laugh when a little white mouse crept out of the straw one afternoon and began to nibble Billy's tail in exactly the same way. She had a shock when she got back to school, though, and the mouse shot out from the end of her sleeve. He scuttled across the floor in the middle of a deportment lesson, making the whole class scream and drop their *Princess Manners for Beginners* with an almighty bang.

Luckily, the mouse found his way back

to the stables, and Grace always put a few extra slices of peach in Billy's bowl for him to share.

The princesses hadn't been allowed to ride their unicorns yet, but Sir Rolling-Trot had taught them how to feed and groom them.

Sometimes Grace braided Billy's thick mane just like her own hair, but mostly she combed it out, free and flowing. Best of all, she loved to brush his long, streaming tail. Billy may not have shone like silver or gleamed like gold, but when Grace was finished with him, he looked handsome and brave.

"Billy is a hearty mountain unicorn," said Sir Rolling-Trot when they were all lined up for inspection one day. "You have him looking just right, Princess Grace. Natural and strong. Splendid work. Well done."

Grace glowed with pride.

Beside her, Precious was tying a sparkly ribbon around Champion's ear. He already had twelve golden pom-poms hanging from his mane and twenty-four silver bows on his tail.

She grinned at the riding teacher, waiting for his praise.

But Sir Rolling-Trot only paused for a moment. "Make sure we can see the unicorn under all those frills," he said.

Then he walked on to compliment Princess Emmeline on her beautiful black mare, whose coat shone like polished ebony.

Precious scowled. "I don't know why you're smiling so happily," she hissed at Grace. "Just because that horse-faced fool said something nice to you. It's the first time any teacher at Tall Towers has said you've done well in anything. I've already had three

Deportment Merits and been Ballroom Dancer of the Week. So there."

It was true. Grace had not found the other lessons easy.

"I feel at home here in the stables." She shrugged.

"Probably because it reminds you of your smelly old castle!" cried Precious, roaring with laughter.

But the smile soon disappeared from her face.

Sir Rolling-Trot was handing out thirteen long-handled shovels and thirteen brooms. "Today we will learn to muck out our unicorns," he said.

"What?" Precious threw her shovel to the ground with a furious clatter. "You don't mean you want us to clean up the . . . You can't actually expect us to . . ."

"Yes, my dear," chuckled the riding master. "I'm afraid I mean just that. It is time to scoop some poop!"

"But we are *princesses*," raged Precious. "*Royal* princesses. Don't you understand that, sir?"

"Indeed I do," said Sir Rolling-Trot calmly. "I have been lucky enough to teach young royals here at Tall Towers for many years. And every Tall Towers princess has learned how to muck out a stall in her first year."

"Surely that's what we have servants for?" said the twins.

"Exactly." Precious kicked her shovel across the yard. "I never have to do anything for myself at home."

"Then you will find this lesson harder than most, my dear," said Sir Rolling-Trot.

"You have a choice. Either pick up your shovel and muck out one stall. Or continue to make a fuss and you'll muck out all thirteen."

"Just you wait until my daddy hears about this," said Precious. But she picked up her shovel, still muttering under her breath.

"What about our dresses?" wailed the twins.

Sir Rolling-Trot pointed toward the tack room, where there was an assortment of blue overalls and long boots.

"I suggest you slip those on, Young Majesties," he said. "Mucking out a stall is rewarding but grubby work."

Grace smiled when she saw everyone dressed in the overalls—she never thought she would see her princess friends looking like this.

Izumi was so tiny she had to roll the legs of her pants into thick, fat folds so she didn't trip over them.

"These are great!" she cried. "I'm going

to get a pair for my painting. I'll never ruin another dress again."

Grace saw that Izumi had placed a sprig of purple lavender in the clip of her overalls.

"That's pretty. We should get some herbs for everyone," said Grace. "They might feel more princessy then."

"Great idea," agreed Scarlet. "The sweet smell will waft under our noses while we work."

Everyone was delighted as Izumi, Scarlet, and Grace returned from the herb trough by the stable gate with sprigs of wild feathery fennel, purple lavender, and green mint.

"A last sniff of summer before the autumn comes," said Sir Rolling-Trot, looking at the big maple trees behind the stables, which were already starting to turn fiery red.

Even the twins were pleased with their posies.

"How splendid!" they cried, poking sprigs of sweet lavender among their curls.

Only Precious refused to take a posy, holding her nose with one hand as she shoveled sulkily with the other.

At last, the stable yard gleamed clean and bright—and the princesses's faces shone with hard work too.

"Well done," said Sir Rolling-Trot when they had washed their hands under the old iron pump. "Now that you have learned to look after your unicorns, you are ready to ride them. Our first lesson will be tomorrow."

CHAPTER NINE
Riding at Last

The next morning, Grace woke up on the floor as usual.

She leapt to her feet and looked out across Coronet Island. It was a beautiful, bright autumn day.

"Perfect for our first ride!" she cheered as Scarlet and Izumi rubbed their sleepy eyes.

As she rummaged in the wardrobe, Grace was a little surprised by her riding outfit. She hadn't looked at it properly since Fairy Godmother Pom found it for her in the

Sewing Tower on the first day.

It was a thick blue coat and a long skirt, and a peaked hat with a veil.

"It's called a riding habit," Izumi explained. She helped Grace to pin a pretty silver brooch across her collar.

Grace pulled on the tall riding boots that the cobbler from the village had made for her. The school and dancing shoes he had brought fit like gloves and were so soft to walk in that Grace felt as if she was floating on air. The soft new shoes had even helped with deportment a little—Grace could now walk all the way around a pillar without *Princess Manners for Beginners* falling to the floor.

But the riding boots were different—they felt strong and secure.

"I could gallop round the world and back in these." She smiled as she clattered down the stairs with Izumi and a nervous-looking Scarlet close behind.

Riding was the first lesson and, to have extra time with the unicorns, they were going to miss breakfast in the Dining Tower and have toast and tea in the stable yard.

Scarlet was pale and quiet.

Grace's pulse was racing with excitement, like the hooves of a galloping horse.

She had spent hours at home riding an imaginary unicorn made from an old mop. Now she grabbed a broom from among a pile of fallen leaves.

"Giddyup," she said, trying to make Scarlet laugh so that she would feel better.

Scarlet smiled.

"Bit of a prickly mane, though," said Grace, patting the bristles on the end of the brush.

"You're such a baby," said Precious, striding

past. "I don't know why you're so excited anyway. You're bound to fall off."

Precious is probably right, thought Grace. She couldn't even balance on a wall without toppling over. But she couldn't get nervous now—not when she had promised Scarlet everything would be all right.

"Hop on!" she cried, gesturing to her friend to join her on the back of the broom.

"Whoa!" Scarlet said, clinging to Grace's waist as they charged across the yard.

"See," Grace laughed. "You're riding already."

"It won't be anything like that," said Precious as the two girls swung their legs off the broom and propped it against the stable wall.

"True," said Grace, squeezing Scarlet's hand. "We probably won't be allowed to gallop quite as fast as that on the first day."

"I meant that we will be riding sidesaddle, of course," sneered Precious, pointing at the unicorns, all tacked up and standing in a line. "Tall Towers princesses always do."

"Sidesaddle?" Grace gulped. Suddenly the long skirt on the riding habit made sense. She had never dreamed they would ride the unicorns this way.

"What did you think you were?" laughed Precious. "A farm boy on a cart horse?"

When they had drunk their tea and eaten slices of hot buttered toast, the princesses led the unicorns into the beautiful indoor Dressage Hall. It was more like a grand ballroom than a riding school, with white marble pillars and three glistening crystal chandeliers hanging from the ceiling by red velvet ropes. Instead of a carpet or floorboards like a ballroom, though, the floor of the Dressage Hall was covered in thick sawdust to protect the animals' hooves.

At least the ground will be soft if we fall off, thought Grace.

A dozen grooms appeared, and along with Sir Rolling-Trot, they helped the princesses to mount their unicorns.

Billy jiggled his head with excitement as he felt Grace's weight drop into the saddle.

"He has spirit, this one, Your Majesty," muttered the groom.

Grace was sure she would feel much better if her legs were on either side of the saddle.

She had sat on some of the old yaks at home that way. With both legs perched on the same side of the saddle, Grace felt as if she was balancing on a slippery, swaying piano stool with nothing behind her and nothing in front.

Beneath her, Billy was prancing from side to side, like a goat on springs.

Grace toppled over backward and landed on the soft sawdust.

Plop!

"Whoops-a-daisy," said Sir Rolling-Trot as Grace scrambled on again with the help of a groom. "That's the spirit!" He smiled. "Always get right back in the saddle if you can."

Grace did her best to stay cheerful as she fell off three more times in a row. At last, she managed to complete a whole circle of the Dressage Hall, clinging tight to the saddle.

"That's better," said Sir Rolling-Trot.

Some of the other princesses had fallen off too. Visalotta sat in the middle of the sawdust, looking very surprised to be there. Izumi had tumbled once when Beauty shied. But Scarlet sat straight as a ballerina, as if she had been riding sidesaddle all her life. Only her wide eyes gave away how terrified she was.

Why can't I be more like Scarlet? She's always so elegant, thought Grace. *Or even like Precious . . .* A wisp of jealousy rose inside her as she wobbled and grabbed at Billy's mane.

Precious had taken riding lessons on ponies at home. She was turning round in her saddle, grinning at everyone as she steered Champion in a figure eight.

"Let's all try trotting now," said Sir Rolling-Trot.

Plop!

Grace fell off again.

★ ★ ★

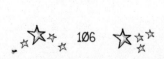

By the time the lesson was over, Grace had fallen twelve times.

"I wouldn't worry. That's the sign of a good rider." Sir Rolling-Trot smiled, patting Billy as he was unsaddled in the stable yard. "I am impressed by your spirit, Grace. You got back up every time you fell. Not a lot of young princesses would do that."

"Thank you." Grace tried to smile. She knew Sir Rolling-Trot was being kind, but it didn't make her feel any better. She had longed to ride ever since she was tiny, always pretending in her games that she was a champion horsewoman. Now that she finally had the chance to sit on a real unicorn, she had to do it sidesaddle, like a dainty princess. She couldn't stay on for more than five minutes.

"Pity you are no better at riding than you are at curtsying," laughed Precious as she

snapped her fingers for a groom to come
and unsaddle Champion.

"Oh, go stick your head in the muck
heap," snapped Grace. The words were out
of her mouth before she could stop herself.

"I'm sorry. I didn't mean to be rude,"
she said, turning to the riding master. She
didn't want him to think that she wasn't a
proper princess. She tugged the veil of her
hat down over her face so Precious wouldn't
see her blush.

Rip!

Grace yanked so hard that the thin netting
tore free from the hat and floated up into
the air. A gust of wind caught it and blew
it over the maple trees.

"Oh no," gasped Grace.

"Looks like it's heading for the beach,"
said Sir Rolling-Trot.

Grace watched, amazed, as the dark square

of netting flew over the meadow and down toward the sand. "It's blown so far away already," she said.

"You'd better go and fetch it, then, hadn't you," said Precious. "Before it goes any farther and you end up looking even more scruffy than before."

Grace couldn't stand it anymore.

"All right, I will," she said. And before her friends could stop her, she climbed up onto the gate and scrambled onto Billy's broad back, one leg on either side, as if she was on a bicycle.

"I'll ride down to the beach and get it right now," she said.

"You can't sit like that!" Precious cried. "Only boys sit like that. Tell her, Sir Rolling-Trot."

The other princesses gasped. But Sir Rolling-Trot just laughed. "Good for you,

Princess Grace. You go and fetch that veil. I'll tell Flintheart . . . I mean, Fairy Godmother Flint, that you'll be a little late for deportment class."

Grace couldn't believe what she had done. Now that she was up on Billy's back, she didn't really know what to do.

But as Sir Rolling-Trot opened the gate, she squeezed Billy with her legs, and he shot forward with a rollicking bound.

Grace grabbed his mane, but she didn't fall off.

"Good boy," she whispered.

As Billy bounced away across the meadow, Grace knew she didn't look elegant . . . but she felt as if she was really riding at last. The minute Billy's hooves felt the soft sand, he began to canter.

The beach was deserted, just a few swooping seagulls, and the princess and her unicorn charging toward the distant lighthouse.

Grace felt herself fit into Billy's rolling rhythm as he sped along. Cantering bareback was actually easier than trotting.

"Giddyup!" she cried, just as she had done a million times in her games at home. She wasn't afraid at all. The wind whipped her hair, and Billy splashed through the edge of the waves, sending sea spray flying up behind them.

"Whee!" whooped Grace. For the first time in her whole life she didn't feel clumsy. She couldn't trip, because her feet weren't on the ground; Billy's legs were doing the work for her. All she had to do was cling tight and encourage him. . . .

She pulled gently on his mane, steering him toward something dark and blue she could see fluttering along the sand.

"My veil!" she cried, slowing Billy to a trot.

But she couldn't bear to get down from his back, not even for a moment. So she walked him over to a cluster of trees at the edge of the dunes. She snapped a dead branch from above her head and broke off the twigs until she had a long, straight stick like a knight's lance. Then she charged back down the beach and speared the veil in one go.

"Got it!" She grinned as Billy leapt

forward and thundered back to the school like a knight's charger.

By the time Grace had brushed Billy down, fed him some hay, and seen him tucked safely into his stable, she had missed her entire deportment lesson.

"Never mind," Sir Rolling-Trot laughed. "From what I saw, you learned quite a lot about keeping your back straight and your head high down there on the beach. I said you'd be a good rider . . . and you are."

"Thank you." Grace flung her arms around Billy's neck. "It was the most exciting thing I have ever done."

"That breath of sea air did you a world of good." Sir Rolling-Trot chuckled. "Much better than standing around with a book on your head, eh?"

"Oh yes," agreed Grace. "Much better."

CHAPTER TEN
The Golden Princess

The next morning, Grace was not so lucky.

"Double deportment," she groaned, checking the timetable scroll on the First Year Common Room wall.

Grace picked up her copy of *Princess Manners for Beginners* and balanced it carefully on her head.

"We're supposed to have our curtsies perfect for today," said Scarlet.

"Today?"

Thud!

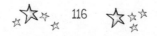

Princess Manners for Beginners fell to the floor.

"Come on," said Izumi, grabbing the book. "We'd better not be late. Flintheart was furious you missed her lesson yesterday."

"It was awful," agreed Scarlet. "I had to give her the note from Sir Rolling-Trot. I thought steam was going to come out of her ears."

"Good thing she didn't see me charging down the beach on Billy-the-Thunderbolt." Grace giggled. "Or she'd have boiled over like a cauldron."

They slipped into the ballet studio just as Fairy Godmother Flint was clapping her hands to begin.

"Backs straight. Books on your heads," she ordered. "Good of you to join us, Princess Grace. No items of lost clothing to find on the beach today? A handkerchief in the rose gardens, perhaps? A lost sock in the meadow?"

The class giggled.

Grace shook her head.

Thud.

Princess Manners for Beginners crashed to the floor. Grace had forgotten it was up there again.

"Dear me," said Flintheart coldly. "I see you still have a very long way to go before you will be ready for the tournament, Grace. It is a pity, because Lady DuLac is coming to visit our class this morning to watch a demonstration of curtsies." She clapped her hands again, gesturing to the girls to curtsy with the books firmly on their heads.

"The headmistress is coming here for a very special reason," the fairy godmother continued. "She is going to pick one of you to be the Golden Princess at the tournament. The girl who is chosen will lead the parade wearing a long gold dress. At the end of the jousting, she will curtsy and present a trophy to the winning knight."

"Oh dear, I hope it's not me," said Scarlet, looking worried.

The other princesses were grinning brightly.

"It will be a great honor for whoever is picked, of course," said Flintheart.

Precious was sticking her nose in the air and smiling smugly as if she was sure that she would be chosen.

Grace's shoulders slumped. There was no chance she would be picked to be the Golden Princess. But she wished she could have a few more days before she had to show Lady DuLac her disastrous curtsy.

Crash.

Princess Manners for Beginners fell to the floor yet again.

Grace was scrabbling around to find it, her bottom sticking out from under a row of little gold chairs, when Lady DuLac swept into the studio.

"Good morning, Headmistress," chorused the girls.

"Oops." Grace stood up so fast that the chair came with her, balancing on her head like a lopsided golden crown.

"Good morning, Young Majesties." Lady DuLac smiled as Grace fought to pull the chair from her ears. "As I am sure Fairy Godmother Flint has explained, I am going to pick one of you to represent Tall Towers as our Golden Princess at the joust. After all, you young First Years are the future of our school."

"Pick me, pick me!" cried Precious, flicking her golden ringlets.

"Or us!" cried the twins. "We could do it together. Wouldn't that be adorably cute?"

Lady DuLac held up her hands. "I wish I could choose you all," she said. "Unfortunately, there is only one trophy to present."

"Let us show the headmistress our curtsies," said Fairy Godmother Flint.

Grace edged toward the back of the room.

"Sorry," she mouthed as she collided with Scarlet, who was trying to hide too.

"You should go to the front," Grace whispered. "Your curtsy is the most graceful in the class."

Scarlet shook her head. "I get terrible stage fright. I'd hate to stand up on my own in front of all those people at the joust."

In the end, it was hopeless to try to hide, as Fairy Godmother Flint lined them up in the far corner of the room and asked them to cross the floor diagonally, curtsying for Lady DuLac one by one as they reached the center. All it meant was that Grace and Scarlet were now at the back of the line and would be the last to go.

Precious, of course, had pushed herself to the front.

"We want to see a full ceremonial curtsy," said Fairy Godmother Flint. "That means you must sink lower and hold your positions for longer than you normally would."

At least we won't have our books on our heads for once, thought Grace.

"I'll show you all how it's done," crowed Precious.

She performed a beautiful curtsy, and everyone clapped politely as she held her balance close to the floor.

To Grace, all the princesses looked elegant, flowing across the room. But Scarlet seemed almost to float. In spite of her shyness, she didn't rush or stumble.

That just left Grace.

She strode across the room.

When the other princesses walked, there didn't seem to be any sound at all, but Grace could hear the thud of her feet on the wooden studio floor.

Down she bobbed.

The curtsy wasn't too bad. Without *Princess Manners for Beginners* on her head, Grace managed to sweep quite low and hold her position for at least a second or two.

It was only as she came up again that she slipped.

Her spaghetti legs twisted around each other, and she couldn't quite figure out how to untangle them again.

Her arms spun in the air like the branches of a tree in a storm. By a stroke of luck, she managed to stop herself from falling over and instead skidded to the opposite corner of the room.

Everyone clapped, except Precious and the twins.

"Thank you," said Lady DuLac. "What a difficult task it will be to choose between you all."

"But I am the best," whined Precious. "It was obvious."

"Thank you, Precious." Lady DuLac cleared her throat. "Perhaps we should ask Fairy Godmother Flint who she feels are her most promising deportment students."

"Princess Precious has fine posture," said Flintheart. "But Princess Scarlet is the most balletic. She has true talent."

Scarlet looked at the floor and shook her head.

Lady DuLac nodded as if she was thinking about something. "I suspect Princess Scarlet would not welcome this role at the moment," she said. "I do not wish to force anyone to do anything they do not wish to. We will find other challenges for you as you grow in confidence and move on through the school. I know you will do great things for us when you are ready, Princess Scarlet."

Grace squeezed her friend's hand. She knew that in her kind and gentle way, Scarlet did brave things every day already.

"And in that case," said the headmistress, "Precious will be the Golden Princess and award the trophy at the joust."

"Yes!" whooped Precious. She spun into the middle of the room with a triple pirouette. "I knew it would be me."

"But," said Lady DuLac firmly, "I have not been impressed by the way that you have shown off today, Precious. A true princess should be proud of the things she is good at but should never be boastful or laugh at others when they try their best."

"I know that." Precious shrugged as if she wasn't really listening.

"If I hear that you have been showing off or making fun of others again, you will not represent Tall Towers at the tournament," said Lady DuLac. "I will give the job of Golden Princess to somebody else."

CHAPTER ELEVEN
Friendship and Pearls

The days grew colder over the next few weeks as autumn turned to winter. Precious talked of nothing except being the Golden Princess at the tournament. She even tried to get the other princesses to call her "Precious the Golden," but nobody did. Not even the twins.

There were now regular practices for the parade, and the First Year princesses had never been so busy. Yet, between rehearsals, dance classes, deportment, riding, and all their other lessons, friendships grew and flourished.

Grace liked everyone in her class—except her spiteful cousin, of course, and the silly twins, who just encouraged Precious to be mean and copied everything she said. Visalotta seemed distant and bored but not unkind.

Most of all, Grace knew how lucky she was to have found such wonderful friends as Scarlet and Izumi. Scarlet was so gentle and kind. Grace loved the way she would burst into fits of giggles at a moment's notice. But Grace also loved how confident and sure of things Izumi was. Although she was the youngest and smallest princess in the class, she was always true to herself and didn't worry what other people thought. Yet she always noticed what was going on around her too. Her pictures were beautiful and bold, and she carried the little sketchbook wherever she went.

Grace and Izumi made a funny pair as they hurried through the corridors together, one so tall, the other so tiny.

"You look like a skinny beanstalk and a tiny ant," said Precious when she saw them heading to the Sewing Tower one day.

"How hilarious! A beanstalk and an ant," squealed the twins.

Grace and Izumi just laughed, holding hands as they ran to catch up with Scarlet.

The three friends were nearly always together, only separating when Scarlet went to practice her dancing and Izumi disappeared to draw or paint. Grace made sure that she spent time with Billy every day. She was doing well in riding lessons—even sidesaddle didn't seem so tricky after her bareback race down the beach. Precious was furious when Grace was awarded the Best Rider Merit three weeks in a row.

But what Grace loved most of all was to take Billy out riding on her own.

Sir Rolling-Trot came to her in the stables when she was grooming Billy one day.

He coughed politely to get her attention. "I found this old saddle in the back of the tack room," he said. "It needs a bit of a polish, but I thought you might find a use for it."

Grace looked up, expecting to see a sidesaddle—but this one had stirrups on both sides.

"It's a ratty old thing. I think it must have been used by one of the grooms years ago," said Sir Rolling-Trot. "But it might save you sitting bareback if you want to take Billy up to the woods and so forth. So long as you always tell me you're leaving, I don't see any problem with you going for a ride."

"Thank you!" cried Grace. She looked at the dusty old saddle covered in cobwebs and wisps of straw. It was just about the best present she had ever been given.

She polished the saddle until it shone. After that she went riding whenever she could.

The trees were bare now, and snow covered the mountains as winter crept in. But Grace was used to the cold. Fairy Godmother Pom had made her a pair of warm riding breeches. She had the thick hairy cloak she had arrived in, and Billy's own fur grew more shaggy. They didn't mind what the weather was like as long as they were out together exploring.

"Coronet Island is so beautiful," Grace told Izumi and Scarlet as she stood dripping in the dormitory after a particularly rainy ride. "The woods go on for miles, and there are secret towers and caves. We've been right to the edge of the mountains where a great waterfall gushes down, and I've seen Mermaid Beach and the lagoon where we'll swim in the summer term."

"It sounds wonderful," said Izumi. "I'd love to explore."

"Let's all go for a ride together this weekend," said Grace. "It might be too cold for a picnic, but we could take some marshmallows and hot chocolate in a thermos."

"Just so long as there's none of your fluffy fudge," laughed Scarlet.

On Saturday morning, Grace woke up with a bump as she landed on the floor as usual. She hurried to get the others out of bed.

It was a beautiful crisp, clear day. They could see the snowy mountains against the cloudless sky as they trotted out of the stable yard on their unicorns.

They had asked Sir Rolling-Trot for permission to leave early, and no one else was up.

"It's almost as if this is our own private island," said Izumi.

The Tall Towers cook had packed them a little saddlebag each of hot chocolate in a thermos, fresh-baked rolls, and peach jam.

Beauty and Velvet tossed their heads. They seemed excited to be ridden outside the Dressage Hall for a change.

"Come on," said Grace as Billy pawed the ground. "I think these unicorns want to feel the wind in their manes. I know the perfect route. We can get a good gallop along the beach, then walk up through the woods and along the river to eat breakfast."

The ride was beautiful, and the girls laughed and chattered as they went. It felt good to be away from school, without

Precious showing off and the cold glare of Flintheart for a while.

Even Scarlet galloped along the beach at full tilt—although she clung to Beauty's neck and closed her eyes most of the time.

"Goodness," she gasped, her cheeks glowing as they reached the woods and slowed down to a trot. "Knights must be so brave to charge like that in a joust. I can't imagine how my poor cousin Wilbur can stand it."

"We'll see him at the tournament next week," said Izumi.

"It's so soon now," said Grace. "I can't wait to see the horses."

They trotted on along the edge of the river and stopped to eat their breakfast at the gushing falls, which tumbled down from the mountains in a great torrent of splashing water.

"Oh dear," said Izumi. "Those clouds don't look good."

The sky above them was silvery gray now.

"We better hurry," said Scarlet.

"Don't worry," said Grace. "It won't rain. I'm sure of it."

Ten minutes later, they were soaked to the skin. It wasn't just rain either. There were hailstones the size of diamond rings, drumming on their riding hats and sliding like chips of ice down the back of their necks.

By the time they had ridden home and put the unicorns in their stables, they were dripping like soggy dishcloths.

Grace had never seen Scarlet and Izumi look so bedraggled before. Water was squelching over the top of Izumi's boots, and Scarlet's lips were blue.

"But it was so much fun," they all agreed

as they dashed across the courtyard and flung open the door to the Dormitory Tower.

Precious was coming down the stairs.

"Just look at you three," she sneered. "Grace's untidiness must be catching. Now there are three Princess DisGraces instead of one."

"It's only water." Grace shrugged, ignoring her meanness.

"We'll soon dry off," agreed Izumi.

"You really shouldn't spend so much time with Grace," said Precious, grabbing Scarlet by the arm. "You might become as hopeless as she is. You wouldn't want that, would you? She's more like a scarecrow than a princess."

"Come on," said Grace. "Let's go up to the dormitory."

But Scarlet had flushed bright red. Raindrops were running off her nose, and she had a look of fury on her face that Grace had never seen before.

"I've had enough of this. How would you feel if someone spoke to you like that, Precious?" she said.

Precious just laughed.

"In half an hour, we will be dry and clean," said Scarlet, her voice shaking as she spoke. "But you will still be mean and spiteful. You say such terrible things to Grace. I don't know why. If you only took the trouble to get to know her, you'd find out how lovely she is."

"Well said," cheered Izumi.

Grace wanted to hug them both. She knew how much courage it must have taken Scarlet to speak out like that. And she was right about what she said. Grace tried not to show it, but Precious's constant bullying beat against her like a storm of hailstones every day.

Precious poked her finger in Scarlet's face.

"How dare you speak to me like that?" she shrieked. "Little Miss Shy, who isn't brave enough to curtsy to a knight. None of you are even good enough to look at me. I am the best student in the whole class. I am the Golden Princess. I—"

"Be quiet," said Scarlet.

Precious raised her hand.

THWACK!

She slapped Scarlet across the cheek.

"Ow!" Scarlet yelped and stumbled backward.

"Stop!" cried Grace. She tried to grab her cousin's arm.

There was a clatter as the string of beads around Precious's neck broke.

The floor was covered with rolling pearls.

"Now look what you've done!" screamed

Precious. "That necklace belonged to Granny. It's worth more than your father's whole kingdom."

The door to Flintheart's office swung open, and the fairy godmother stepped out. Lady DuLac was with her.

CHAPTER TWELVE
Practice Dress

Flintheart folded her arms. Her face was like thunder. Grace gave Scarlet a reassuring hug.

"It was all Grace's fault," whined Precious. "Scarlet and I had a little bit of a fight. I was only trying to hug and make up. But Grace was clumsy and got in the way as usual. I ended up knocking Scarlet's cheek by mistake. I didn't mean to hit her. It was only because Grace bashed my arm. And now my valuable pearls are broken." She held out the handful of beads that Izumi had gathered from the floor and given her.

"That's not true. That's not how it happened!" cried Scarlet.

"You slapped Scarlet on purpose," said Izumi. "Grace wasn't anywhere near you. And the pearls can be mended easily," she added.

"It's all right," said Lady DuLac, stepping forward and wrapping her own shawl around Scarlet's shivering shoulders. "Fairy Godmother Flint and I heard the whole thing." She patted Scarlet's arm and smiled. "You showed great bravery defending your friend when you thought that someone else's words would hurt her. That takes a different sort of nerve than curtsying to a crowd. Standing up for what is right is the most important sort of courage of all. I am only sorry that you got hurt trying."

Scarlet lifted her head and smiled.

Lady DuLac turned toward Precious. "You have been warned not to show off about your role as Golden Princess, and yet you did. But worse than that, today you behaved in a cruel and most un-princess-like way."

"It wasn't my fault," growled Precious, kicking her pointy gold shoes against the tiles.

"I am afraid you leave me no choice but to take away your role of Golden Princess," said Lady DuLac. "Someone else will have that honor at the tournament."

"You can't do that!" cried Precious. She was actually stamping her feet now. "I'll tell my daddy!"

Grace, Scarlet, and Izumi glanced at each other in shock.

"Perhaps we *should* think of another punishment, Headmistress," said Flintheart, panic rising in her voice. "There is so little time before the tournament."

"But my golden dress has been made and everything!" wailed Precious. "What are you going to do? Get someone stupid like Grace, who can't even curtsy properly?"

Flintheart gasped. "Don't be silly!" she cried. "Grace could not be the Golden Princess."

But Lady DuLac held up her hand. She opened her mouth to speak, then closed it again. She began to pace up and down, drumming her fingers together as if she was trying to make up her mind. A slow smile spread across her face.

"Why not?" she said. "Princess Grace has worked hard and tried her very best since the moment she first arrived at Tall Towers. It is a wonderful idea, Precious. Grace thoroughly deserves to be our new Golden Princess."

"Are you joking?" groaned Precious.

"Me?" Grace nearly collapsed on the ground. "You want *me* to be the Golden Princess, Lady DuLac?"

The next few days passed in a haze.

Precious thumped around in such a rage that nobody dared to go near her. The other princesses were shocked when they heard how she had slapped Scarlet. Most thought it was right that she was no longer the Golden Princess. But Grace knew they were worried about how she would do at the tournament instead.

"Just try not to be too clumsy," squealed the twins.

Grace shuddered. She would have to lead the whole parade and then curtsy to the winning knight. She was representing the

First Years in front of the entire school and their parents.

Flintheart's gray face became white with worry. Grace spent every waking minute practicing her curtsy. She almost had it perfectly . . . until she remembered that she would be wearing a long golden dress.

Grace hadn't even had a chance to try the dress on. Fairy Godmother Pom had attempted to let the hem down, but there just wasn't enough material; Grace was so much taller than Precious. In the end, Fairy Godmother Pom had to send to the mainland for fabric and start all over again.

While Scarlet practiced doing Grace's hair, Izumi spent hours in the Sewing Tower helping to cut and measure and sew.

"It is going to be a beautiful dress," she

told Grace. "The train is as long as the tables in the Dining Tower."

"Really?" Grace gulped. "I trip over my dressing-gown cord. How am I going to manage with a golden train long enough for thirteen princesses to eat their breakfast off of?"

"Don't worry, we'll help you," said Scarlet.

On the night before the tournament, Grace stood in her long white nightdress, and Izumi pinned a bedsheet to the hem and spread it out behind her.

"Hmm. It's not quite as long as the golden dress," she said, checking it with her tape measure. "But it's very close."

"Imagine I am my cousin Wilbur." Scarlet giggled, tucking her ponytail into her collar to make herself look more like a boy. "He has red hair just like me. Now try to curtsy, Grace."

"Congratulations on winning the joust, Sir Wilbur," proclaimed Grace in a booming voice that made Scarlet jump.

"I don't think Wilbur will actually win," she laughed. "He'd probably die of fright if he did."

"Sir." Grace bowed her head, as if Scarlet really was a knight, and stepped backward at the same time, dipping her knee low.

There was a horrible ripping sound.

"Oops," said Grace. "I think I put my foot through the sheet."

"Don't worry." Izumi rushed forward with more pins. "Try again. Take a smaller step back. Nobody will see your feet because of the long dress."

"Like this?" asked Grace, bobbing down a second time.

"That's it!" cried Scarlet as Grace managed a perfect curtsy. "The sheet didn't even bunch up behind you. It will look beautiful with the golden dress."

Grace beamed. "Do you really think it will be as easy as that?" she asked.

"I don't see why not," said Izumi. "Your curtsies are elegant now."

Grace practiced ten more times, and each one was perfect.

"I could never have done it without your help," she said, grabbing Scarlet and Izumi by the hand.

"Try to get a good night's sleep," said Izumi as she unpinned the sheet from the back of Grace's nightdress. "You have nothing to worry about now."

"I'd still be far too nervous to sleep." Scarlet gulped. "Just think of all those people who'll be watching you tomorrow."

"Scarlet, that is *not* helping," whispered Izumi.

But Grace just laughed. "I won't sleep a wink," she said, leaping into bed. "But not because I'm scared. I'm excited. I can't wait to see the huge horses and watch the knights joust. Thanks to my two wonderful best friends, everything is going to be perfect at the tournament. I am going to be the most princessy Golden Princess ever. . . ."

CHAPTER THIRTEEN
The Big Day

In fact, Grace fell asleep the minute her head hit the pillow.

"Wake up!" cried Scarlet in the morning.

"It's time to get out of bed," said Izumi.

"*Out* of bed?" Grace sat up and rubbed her eyes. "You mean I didn't fall out in the night."

She looked down at the hard floor where she woke up every morning.

"I can't believe it!" she said, leaping to her feet and bouncing up and down on her mattress. "This is the first night in my whole life I didn't fall out of bed. Maybe now that I have learned to curtsy, my clumsiness is cured forever."

She sprang down and curtsied low to the floor.

"I think you're right," said Scarlet. "It's a sign."

"And it's a lovely, bright day with a gentle touch of frost. Everything will be perfect," agreed Izumi. "Just so long as you get dressed in time."

"Oh no. You both look beautiful already," said Grace, gesturing to the shimmering silver dresses Scarlet and Izumi were wearing.

"Come on," said Izumi. "I can't wait to see you in the golden dress at last."

They all ran across to the Sewing Tower, and Fairy Godmother Pom welcomed them inside.

"Close your eyes tight, Gracie. No peeking," she said as she opened the wardrobe where the dress was hanging. "I've been up half the night putting the finishing touches on it."

There was a rustle of material, and Grace felt the fairy godmother pull the dress down over her head.

"It's a perfect fit!" cried Izumi.

"Don't open your eyes yet," warned the fairy godmother as she fussed with the long gold train.

"You really do look lovely," said Scarlet. There was a tug as she pulled Grace's hair into a tight ballerina's bun.

"Ready?" Fairy Godmother Pom clapped her hands. "You can look now, Gracie."

Grace opened her eyes and stared into the mirror.

The dress was long and straight, with a

dropped waist and scooped sleeves. It had a fluffy winter collar, and the hem was trimmed with golden velvet.

"It's gorgeous," she gasped. "Thank you. I never dreamed I could look like this."

Grace remembered standing here all those weeks before, the first time she had seen herself in the white school pinafore. Then she had truly felt like a princess. Today, she didn't even feel like a princess. She felt like a queen or an empress in the beautiful golden dress.

"Princess Izumi designed most of it," said Fairy Godmother Pom.

"Thank you, Izumi. You're so smart. And my hair looks great too," she said, hugging Scarlet.

"You all look very elegant," said Fairy Godmother Pom as the three girls stood in front of the mirror together. "But you'd better hurry along. The parents will be arriving soon, and you aren't supposed to be seen before the parade."

"Yes, we mustn't be late, or old Flintheart will have a fit," said Grace, gathering up her dress in great armfuls and secretly wishing that the train wasn't quite so long. "Thank you for everything, Fairy Godmother Pom."

Scarlet and Izumi helped her down the steps of the tower.

"Look. That must be Visalotta's boat," said Izumi as they dashed across the courtyard, holding Grace's golden train high off the ground.

"I heard it was made of real rubies, but I never believed it," said Scarlet.

Grace turned her head to see a sparkling red yacht coming into the harbor below the school. In the winter sunshine, the water twinkled as if it was on fire, but it was only the glow of the jewels.

"Hurry," said Izumi. "We're supposed to be in the waiting room outside the Ceremonial Hall before our parents arrive."

There were other boats close to the island too—white schooners and silver rowing vessels.

Grace heard the roar of an engine and saw her aunt and uncle's huge golden speedboat skim into the harbor behind Visalotta's yacht.

"Quick," she said. "Let's go." The last thing she wanted to do was bump into Precious's parents right now.

But halfway across the courtyard, she heard a booming voice she recognized instantly.

"Grace? Is that you all dressed up?"

She spun around to see her father striding toward her in his best fur cloak and yak-skin boots. His long beard was flying out behind him. Grace had gotten used to how tall and broad he was at home, but here he seemed like a giant.

"Papa!" she cried, running to him in spite of the golden dress.

Grace's little sister, Pip, was there too, trotting after the king, her dark chocolatey hair gathered into two stiff little bunches sticking out from each side of her head. She had a pretty, round face with dimples in her chubby cheeks and a big gappy smile where she had lost one of her baby teeth at the front. Apart from their hazel eyes, the two sisters looked nothing alike.

"Goodness! Golly! Gosh!" Pip dashed forward and flung her arms around Grace's waist. "You look like a real, proper princess," she gasped.

Grace laughed, then picked Pip up and spun her round.

"I've been asked to be the Golden Princess

today. It's a special job at the tournament."
She hugged her father too. It was so good
to see them both after so long.

"And these are my two best friends," she
said, turning to Scarlet and Izumi. She had
told her father all about them in the letters
she wrote home every week.

"Princess Izumi and Princess Scarlet, I
presume," said the king, bowing low as the
girls curtsied.

"Golly!" said Pip again. "They're so
sparkly." She took hold of Grace's hand and
stared up at Scarlet and Izumi as if they had
stepped off the pages of a storybook.

"We have to go, or we'll be in trouble with
our teacher," said Grace, trying to pry Pip's
fingers away. "We'll see you right after the
tournament. I'll show you my unicorn, Billy."

"I wish I was at princess school," sniffed
Pip, still clinging to Grace's hand. "I wish I

had a golden dress as lovely as yours."

"You'll be a student at Tall Towers soon," said Scarlet.

"And you look lovely already," said Izumi, pointing to the little blue-and-white polka-dot frock that Pip was wearing. Grace remembered that it used to belong to her, but it suited Pip much better.

"Gosh!" Pip was so pleased and shy, she grabbed hold of Grace's knees and hid in the folds of her dress.

"We really *do* have to go," said Grace helplessly.

"Take a bit of fudge first," said her father. "Cook made it specially." He opened his handkerchief to reveal a pile of fluffy sweets. "Sorry," he mumbled. "I think they might have gotten a little hairy in the pocket of my cloak."

Grace could see Scarlet and Izumi trying

not to giggle as they remembered the midnight feast on their very first night at Tall Towers. With perfect princess politeness, they each took a piece of the furry fudge from the king's enormous handkerchief.

"Delicious." They smiled.

"Just don't think about hairy caterpillars . . . or dragon dung," Grace whispered as they turned toward school. But before she could walk away, her father caught hold of her sleeve.

"Wait." He put his arm around her shoulders as the others ran inside.

"I am so proud of you, Grace," he said. "You look so elegant and graceful in that golden dress. You're growing up to be a proper princess. I know it can't always be easy without your mother around. But she would be so happy if she could see you today."

Grace felt a glow inside her. Her father normally talked to her about yak farming.

Or he held her upside down and tickled her. Or he told her gory legends about Cragland's past and the terrible bloodthirsty creatures that had lived and died there long ago. He had never actually given her a compliment before. It made her blush as red as Visalotta's ruby boat.

"Thank you, Papa," she said.

Now that she had learned to curtsy properly, she wouldn't make a fool of herself at the tournament, and he would be even more proud of her.

At that moment, a king and queen—who must have been Visalotta's parents, judging by their enormous diamond crowns—appeared in the entrance to the courtyard. Precious's parents were just behind them.

"I say, Queen Greya, is that your daughter?" boomed Visalotta's father over his shoulder. "She's dressed as the Golden Princess."

"Oh yes." Precious's mother, Queen Greya, bustled into the courtyard. "Precious is always chosen for the most important honors," she said.

But Aunt Greya's face fell when she saw that it was not her daughter in the golden gown.

"Who are you?" she roared. "And why are you wearing that dress?"

It was obvious Precious hadn't told her parents that she wasn't going to be the Golden Princess anymore.

Grace gulped. Did she really look so different that even her aunt didn't recognize her?

"It's me," she said, curtsying low to the ground without a single wobble. "Your niece Grace."

"Grace?" Queen Greya's eyes opened wide with shock. "I didn't recognize you looking so . . . so . . ."

"Clean?" said Grace's uncle Herbert.

"You do know this princess, then?" Visalotta's mother smiled.

"She's just my sister's girl," mumbled Queen Greya. "She's nobody."

Grace felt a flash of anger. *I am* not *a nobody,* she thought. *I am a proper princess now—a Golden Princess. For today, at least.*

"Pleased to meet you," she said, curtsying to Visalotta's mother. "My name is Princess Grace."

Her father stepped forward and bowed too.

"Grace is *my* fine young daughter," he said proudly.

Grace flung her arms around him. "I've got to go," she whispered. "But I won't let you down, Papa, I promise."

She grabbed the train on her dress, hitched it over her arm, and dashed inside like a charging bull.

CHAPTER FOURTEEN
The Steps

Grace flew into the waiting room outside the Ceremonial Hall with only a second to spare.

Just a moment later, Fairy Godmother Flint swept in.

Grace smiled with relief at Izumi and Scarlet. She was still panting for breath and felt sure her face was bright red from running with the heavy train of the dress scooped up in her arms.

"I shouldn't need to remind you all, this

is a very important day for Tall Towers," said Flintheart, scanning the room. "Please take hold of the items you will carry in the parade."

The other princesses each lifted a brightly colored flag on a golden pole. There were yellow flags, orange flags, green and blue ones. They were decorated with dragons, leaping stags, swans, or unicorns. Each flag represented a different knight taking part in the tournament.

Grace did not have a flag to hold, as it was the Golden Princess's job to carry the trophy that would be awarded to the winning knight. She caught her breath as she lifted the heavy gold cup into the air.

This was it. Her big day had arrived. She had been so busy getting dressed and seeing Pip and her father that she hadn't really had time to feel nervous yet. But now, even though she knew she could curtsy, tiny butterflies were starting to swirl in her stomach.

What was is it Scarlet had said last night?

Her friend's soft, worried voice rang clearly in Grace's head: *"Just think of all those people who'll be watching you."*

Grace's palms were starting to sweat, but she didn't dare to wipe them on the golden dress. The cup slipped a little in her grasp and clanged against the edge of a table.

"Imagine if *someone* in our class made a mess of the parade," squealed the twins. "Wouldn't that be awful?"

"*Who* would do a thing like that?" asked Precious nastily. "If we don't make a good impression, it will bring shame on the whole school, won't it, Fairy Godmother?"

Grace knew they meant her.

"It most certainly will." Flintheart was

scowling at Grace too. "I will not tolerate clumsiness or mistakes today."

She gestured to the large wooden doors that led from the little waiting room to the grand Ceremonial Hall. "Every parent in the school—royal kings and queens of great importance—are waiting for us to enter through those doors and lead them down to Silver Meadow, where they will be seated to watch the joust," she said. "Our procession will be calm and orderly. We will walk along the red carpet down the middle of the hall as if we are floating. As we pass, we will curtsy to the waiting kings and queens, who will follow us down the steps to the garden."

"Steps?" Grace grabbed Scarlet's arm. "I had completely forgotten there would be steps."

"There are about twenty, I think," murmured Scarlet, looking worried.

"Twenty-four," whispered Izumi. "I counted them one day when I was sketching."

"Twenty-four?" Grace forgot to whisper. The thought of trying to glide gracefully down twenty-four steps without tripping over the golden train was too much.

"I am sorry some students feel they are so special and important that they don't need to listen to instructions," said Flintheart, stepping toward Grace. "Has wearing the golden dress gone to your head, Young Majesty? It is not too late to change again and get someone else to wear the dress, you know."

"Pick me!" squealed Trinket.

"No, me!" squawked Truffle.

"I'm sorry," said Grace. "I really am listening." The trophy she was holding weighed as much as the full buckets of water she carried across the yard for Billy. It would make walking down the steps even harder. But she didn't dare complain.

"As I was saying before I was so rudely interrupted," continued Flintheart, "you will walk slowly, calmly, and *gracefully* down the steps, and then lead the way to Silver Meadow. Princess Grace will be in front with the trophy. The rest of you, carrying the flags, will be behind. I want to see shoulders back and necks straight, as if a book was balanced on your heads."

Grace thought of how many times *Princess Manners for Beginners* had crashed to the floor in deportment class.

"Once the parents are seated in the stands around the meadow, the tournament will begin," said Fairy Godmother Flint. "All that will remain then is for Princess Grace to curtsy to the winning knight and present the trophy when the joust is over."

"I still don't understand why *she* gets to be the Golden Princess," huffed Precious. "Lady DuLac only asked Grace because she felt sorry for her . . . because Grace is so bad at everything."

There was a gasp from some of the other princesses. Even for Precious, this was cruel.

Grace felt as if she had been slapped. Her legs wobbled under the golden dress. But she wasn't going to let Precious ruin this special day. Not when Pip and her father had looked so proud.

"Places, please," said Fairy Godmother Flint.

Grace threw back her shoulders and marched boldly to the front of the line. She could hear the murmur of voices as the kings and queens gathered in the Ceremonial Hall.

Precious and Visalotta were just behind her. Then Scarlet and Izumi. Then Rosamond and Juliette, Latisha and Martine, followed by Christabel and Emmeline. Then, last of all, the twins, who were furious to be at the very back of the line.

"It is simply not fair," Grace heard them moan.

A trumpet sounded. The doors were flung open. Grace stepped forward.

The Ceremonial Hall was crowded with kings and queens from every kingdom. They all fell silent as Grace led the parade of First Years through the doors.

"Shoulders back, head straight," Grace told herself.

She turned first to the left and then to the right, curtsying perfectly as she made her way along the red carpet with her train flowing behind her. The other princesses followed with their flags. They walked on either side of the long train as if it was a golden river flowing between them.

Although the hall was packed with royal visitors, Grace could see that many more were waiting outside, lining the steep stairs to the garden.

She spotted Lady DuLac standing by the open doors with beautiful, raven-haired Princess Ebony, who was head girl. Beyond them, Grace could see the huge figure of her father and tiny Pip on the top step. Precious's parents stood opposite them.

"One foot in front of the other, that's all it takes," Grace whispered under her breath.

Then she was there, standing on the top of the steps, right in front of Lady DuLac.

"Only twenty-four little steps," she told herself. "Just do not stumble."

Grace stepped down the first two stairs perfectly.

"That's it," she said inside her head. "Easy."

She cleared two more steps. It was going to be all right.

"If I do not stumble, I will not trip. If I do not trip, I will not fall . . . ," she whispered.

"I thought you'd be flat on your bum by now," hissed Precious in her ear.

Grace wobbled. She felt something roll underneath her shoe. Her foot slipped forward as if she was suddenly on a pair of roller skates.

"Ahhhh . . . ," Grace heard herself scream.

The huge gold trophy flew through the air.

The world tipped on its head.

Grace gasped. She was tumbling, rolling, falling helplessly down the steps.

"No!" she cried.

The great golden dress ballooned like a parachute behind her.

CHAPTER FIFTEEN
Running Away

Splat!

Grace landed at the bottom of the steps. The long gold dress flew up over her head.

The crowd gasped. Some giggled.

"Look! You can see her knickers," squealed the twins.

Grace desperately pulled the dress down. Her eyes were stinging with shame. She couldn't bear to look up.

"I—I'm sorry. I don't know what

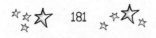 181

happened," she said, trying to smooth the golden dress flat over her knees.

Her cheeks were burning, and her hands shook.

At last, she raised her head.

Everyone was staring at her, their mouths open wide.

She saw her father on the steps above.

His face was as red as a raspberry.

Pip had buried herself in his cloak.

"You tripped over your own big feet, that's all," sneered Precious. "What a disgrace." She had a little, secret grin on her face as if this was what she had been waiting for all along.

Scarlet and Izumi had turned away. Their heads were bowed down, almost as if they were searching for something under their feet.

Grace felt sure they were too embarrassed to look her in the eye.

Fairy Godmother Flint appeared on the steps behind them, her face as dark as thunder.

But it was Lady DuLac who spoke. Her voice was quiet and calm. "Are you hurt, my dear?"

Grace shook her head.

"Good. That's the main thing," said the headmistress gently. "Nothing else matters."

Grace felt her lip wobble. She had wanted so much to impress Lady DuLac. Now the headmistress's kindness was far worse than being shouted at.

She wanted to explain how it had felt as if the ground had suddenly started to roll beneath her feet. She wanted to turn back time so that she could be standing at the top of the steps again, a perfect princess in a golden dress. But she knew it was hopeless. Everything was ruined.

Grace struggled to her feet, hitched up the dress, and ran. Tears were streaming down her face as she hurtled around the corner of the Ceremonial Hall.

"Why am I always so clumsy?" she wailed.

She stumbled on toward the stables, desperate to bury her face in Billy's mane.

But as she turned the corner, she saw

that the field where the unicorns normally grazed was filled with tents. The knights were getting ready for the tournament. Horses were tethered, saddles were being polished, and suits of armor hung like washing from the trees.

The knights were so busy with their preparations that they didn't notice the sobbing princess as she blundered between the tents.

And Grace did not notice the sharp lance lying in her path.

The pointed end of the weapon caught in the long fabric of her dress.

Rrrrip! Grace was still running when she heard the sound.

She looked around and saw with horror that the bottom half of the dress and the shimmering train had been torn clean off.

"Oh no!" Now, instead of a golden ball gown, it looked as if she was wearing a tattered smock. Grace tugged hard, trying to pull the shredded fabric down below her knees as she staggered on across the field. Tears were streaming down her face.

She could never go back to the tournament like this. It was bad enough she had made a mess of the whole parade. Everyone had seen her polka-dot knickers—which still weren't the regulation white ones. Now the golden dress was ruined too.

Grace sped around the side of a bright, striped tent.

The stable was in sight and—

Bam!

She collided with a knight in a full suit of armor.

"Ouch."

Grace leapt up and down clutching her foot.

But the knight came off far worse.

"Wh-whoa," he cried as he toppled over backward and tumbled down the slope.

Dong!

He landed against the high wall in front of the stables, and his armor clanged like a ringing bell.

"I'm so sorry." Grace rushed down the slope after him. "I wasn't looking where I was going. Let me help you—"

"Go away. You're dangerous. Don't come anywhere near me," a dazed voice echoed from inside the helmet.

The knight clattered to his feet, swaying dizzily from side to side. "Just stay over there and—whoa." He tried to steady himself but bashed into the wall again.

Clang!

Now the knight staggered sideways and fell into a ditch.

"I promise I won't hurt you," said Grace,

clambering down into the muddy ditch beside him. "You have to stay still until your head stops spinning."

"But I can't stay still, can I? I'm supposed to joust in a minute," said the knight, pulling off his helmet.

Grace saw that he was just a boy. Not much older than her. He had pale skin and a shock of familiar flame-red hair.

"Goodness. You're not Wilbur, are you?" she gasped.

"Yes, I am." His eyes were wide and frightened. "How did you know?" He looked her up and down. The ragged dress was dripping with mud. "Are you some sort of witch who can read minds or something?"

Grace laughed. "I'm Princess Grace. I'm best friends with your cousin Scarlet. I recognized you by your hair."

"Oh. That's good. I thought you might

want to cast a spell on me." A look of relief flooded over Wilbur's face. Grace wanted to laugh. He seemed just as nervous as Scarlet. "Of course, I knew you weren't a witch really." He blushed. "I think I'm a bit confused. I must have gotten quite a bang rolling around inside that suit of armor."

"And it was all my fault," groaned Grace. "I should have been looking where I was going. Then I frightened you." Her bad day had just gotten worse. On top of everything else, she had nearly knocked out Scarlet's cousin.

"I should have been looking too," he said kindly. "The truth is I was composing a tune in my head."

"A tune?" Grace asked.

"Yes. It went something like this." Wilbur picked up his helmet as if it was a drum and began to beat out a rhythm with his fingers.

Dum de-de dum . . .

But suddenly a terrible voice boomed across the field. "WILBUR! WHERE ARE YOU?"

Grace and Wilbur were still hidden in the deep ditch, so no one could see them. But Wilbur's fingers stopped drumming and his face turned as white as lace.

"Oh no. That's Squire Bellows. It must be time to mount Thunder already."

"Thunder?" asked Grace.

"He's my horse. A terrifying great brute." Wilbur shivered. "But at least he knows what he's doing."

"Don't you like jousting?" asked Grace.

"No. I always fall off in the first two minutes, and I'm terrified of horses." Wilbur tried to get to his feet but quietly sank down again. Grace couldn't tell if he was still dizzy or just scared.

"I want to be a musician, really," he said. "I made a deal with my father that I would train with Squire Bellows and learn to be a knight for a whole year. After that, my father promised I could go to the Royal Musicians Academy and study there. It's all I've ever really wanted to do."

"How wonderful," said Grace. "When is your year with Squire Bellows over?"

"Yesterday," sighed Wilbur. "That's the whole problem. He hasn't realized the time is up, and I'm too scared to tell him."

"WILBUR! WHERE ARE YOU?" The squire's voice blasted across the field again.

"Oh no." Wilbur struggled to his feet.

"You can't go anywhere," said Grace as he wobbled from side to side. "You're still dizzy. You certainly can't ride a horse."

"I have to," said Wilbur. "It's a matter of honor." He buried his head in his hands.

"Honor is very important to knights, you know. Squire Bellows has worked so hard getting Thunder ready for this tournament, I didn't have the heart to tell him I should have left yesterday."

"What will you do?" asked Grace.

"I'll ride in the joust, and then as soon as it's over, I can set off for the Royal Musicians Academy."

"But you *can't* ride," said Grace. Wilbur was swaying dangerously. "You need to see a doctor."

"Do you really think so?" Wilbur's eyes grew wide with panic. "I do feel *very* strange." He slumped down on the grass and buried his head in his hands again. "If I don't ride, the joust might have to be canceled," he groaned. "There won't be enough knights to take part. I'll let everyone down."

No matter how scared or dizzy he felt, Grace

knew Wilbur was determined to do the right thing. But she could clearly see he was terrified. His voice was shaking, and his pale cheeks had turned sickly green.

"I'll just have to ride," he said firmly. "There's nothing else to do."

"Unless . . ." A wonderful, exciting idea shot through Grace's mind like a bolt of lightning. She picked up the helmet from where it lay in the ditch and slipped it over her head.

"I can ride for you!" she cried, her voice sounding strange as it echoed through the helmet. "It's my fault you fell over. I've already ruined the parade. If you don't ride, the tournament will be ruined too."

"B-but . . . you can't do that!" spluttered Wilbur.

"Why not? You're not even supposed to be a knight anymore," said Grace.

"I was a pretty hopeless one anyway," groaned Wilbur. "I find it so frightening when the other knights charge at me."

"I'd love to charge like a knight." Grace grinned. "Just once, at least. It is not the sort of thing a princess usually gets to do."

"WILBUR!" The squire's voice was getting closer and closer.

"Quick," said Grace. "Climb out of your armor. Then you go to the hospital tent, and I'll ride in the joust. It's the best way to save the tournament."

CHAPTER SIXTEEN
The Tournament

Safely disguised as a bold knight, Grace clanked back around the side of the stripy tent. She was glad that the long train had been ripped off the golden dress. Otherwise, she would never have been able to fit inside the suit of armor at all.

Her mouth felt dry as she peered out of the metal visor, which came down like a narrow letter box over her eyes. She was surprised how clearly she could see out. Yet no one would have any idea who was hidden beneath the helmet.

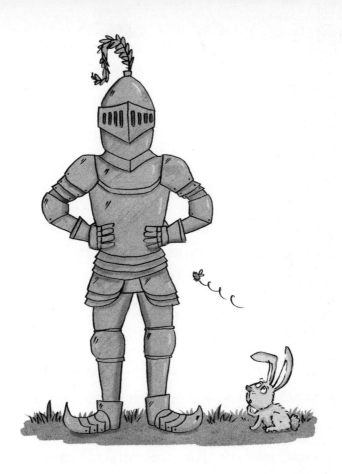

"THERE YOU ARE, WILBUR. WHERE HAVE YOU BEEN, BOY?" A huge mountain of a man with a bristly black mustache strode toward her. He had a black leather patch over one eye and a deep scar under the other. It was Squire Bellows for sure.

No wonder Wilbur is scared of him, thought Grace. Her own heart was pounding, and she was sure Scarlet would have fainted clean away.

"COME ALONG, THEN, LAD," he boomed. From inside her helmet, Grace saw that his teeth were as chipped and cracked as broken plates. "I'VE GOT THUNDER SADDLED UP AND READY TO GO."

A stableboy led a huge black charger toward them. The horse skittered sideways and whinnied, flaring his nostrils like a dragon. Grace wondered if she had made a terrible mistake. But she couldn't run away now. Not in a suit of armor. And she had promised to help Wilbur and save the joust.

"STEADY, THUNDER," warned the squire, patting the beast on its huge flank.

Then he picked Grace up as if she and the armor weighed no more than a loaf of bread and plonked her in the saddle.

"GET GOING, SIR KNIGHT," he roared. "THE CONTEST HAS BEGUN."

"B-but," mumbled Grace through her visor.

"NO TIME TO ARGUE, YOUNG FELLOW," snapped Squire Bellows. He threw Grace a lance and slapped Thunder soundly on the rump. "KNOCK 'EM DOWN, LAD. KNOCK 'EM DOWN, WILBUR."

"I'll try my best," squealed Grace as the horse reared up and galloped toward the joust.

The rules of the joust were simple. Grace had to wield the great lance and knock other knights off their horses. She must topple them first, before they could unseat her.

A knight on a gray horse was charging toward her already, waving his lance like an enormous sword.

Grace tried for a moment to pull Thunder

round and flee. Her plan had been crazy. She couldn't fight like this. But it was no good. Thunder was determined to charge forward. There was no choice but to joust.

I can do this, thought Grace. *I know I can.*
She was good at knocking things down . . .
very good!

She swooshed her lance through the air.

"Ahhhh!"

The knight on the gray horse unbalanced and tumbled to the ground.

Then a fat knight with a long green feather in his helmet charged forward.

Grace swiped her lance in front of her as if it was a pitchfork and she was shoveling dung in the stable yard.

Crash.

The knight with the green feather was gone too.

The crowd leapt to their feet and cheered wildly for the tough little rider on the fine black horse.

"BY GUM, WILBUR. I HAVE NEVER SEEN YOU RIDE LIKE THIS." Squire Bellows's voice rose above the noise.

"How brave he is!" whooped the spectators. "How fast he knocks the others down!"

Safe inside her armor, Grace did feel brave.

She felt strong and fearless as her long legs gripped the saddle and her arms waved the lance in the air.

Beneath her, Thunder swerved and spun. Wilbur was right. The horse knew exactly what he was supposed to do.

He's magnificent, thought Grace.

With no more than a gentle tug on his reins, Thunder was ready to turn and charge again.

"Good boy!" cried Grace, leaning forward to pat him gently with her enormous iron glove.

Riding the big black charger was really no different from the times she had galloped Billy through the woods or along the beach.

Bam!

Another knight fell.

"Thank goodness I am not doing this sidesaddle," laughed Grace. "They would have knocked me down like a china ornament."

Bam!

Another knight rolled in front of her, rattling across the ground like an old tin can.

"Who's clumsy now?" Grace grinned. And—*crash!*—she knocked the last and fastest of the knights to the ground.

The crowd went wild.

Grace flung her arms round Thunder's neck. "Thank you," she breathed.

"The contest is won!" cried Sir Rolling-Trot, leaping out of the umpire's chair, where he had been watching to check that none of the knights broke the rules.

"WHAT A CHAMPION!" proclaimed Squire Bellow, lifting Grace down from her horse.

"Well done, Cousin Wilbur!" cried Scarlet from the First Year seats.

Grace could see her father and Pip

cheering in the front row of the stands, though they had no idea that it was her inside the suit of armor, of course.

Oh dear, thought Grace. *Now what should I do?*

She had never meant to *win* the joust.

"What a wonderful tournament this has been," said Lady DuLac, stepping onto the grass. Her gaze rested for a moment on Fairy Godmother Flint and the First Years. "Where is Grace?" she asked. "Hasn't she come back yet? She needs to present the trophy now."

Grace's face felt hot inside the helmet. Everyone would think she was very spoiled to have run away like that and not come back.

"Princess Precious will present the trophy instead," said Flintheart calmly. "Since Princess Grace appears to have vanished . . . along with the golden dress."

Grace saw her father and Pip exchange a worried glance. Scarlet and Izumi were looking in every direction, trying to spot her.

If only they knew that she was here, inside the armor. But she couldn't show herself. She had to keep Wilbur's secret safe.

Precious was curtsying to the crowd with an enormous grin on her face. She was clearly delighted that Grace had vanished and she got to award the trophy after all.

"WHATEVER IS THE MATTER WITH YOU, BOY?" Squire Bellows slapped Grace so hard on the back of her armor that her teeth rattled. "TAKE YOUR HELMET OFF WHEN A PRINCESS APPROACHES."

Precious was gliding across the grass toward them.

"I can't," coughed Grace, trying to make

her voice sound gruff like a boy's. She held on to her helmet desperately. She was sure that everyone could hear her heart beating against the armor. "I'm too shy," she whispered, thinking that was exactly how Wilbur would feel.

Precious held out the trophy. "Congratulations, brave knight." She smiled and curtsied low to the ground.

"LET THE PEOPLE SEE YOUR FACE, MY BOY!" cried Squire Bellows. "YOU SHOULD BE PROUD OF A RIDE LIKE THAT."

Pop!

He pulled the helmet off Grace's head.

The crowd gasped.

Quickly, Grace tried to duck down inside the armor. But it was hopeless.

"I say, is that you, Grace?" Sir Rolling-Trot

said, jumping out of his chair again. He slapped his sides and laughed. "Well, I never. You are the winning knight!"

"WHAT THE BLAZES IS GOING ON? WHERE IS WILBUR?" thundered Squire Bellows.

"You mean I just curtsied . . . to Grace?" Precious screamed. "That is *so* embarrassing."

The crowd roared with laughter—especially the First Year princesses.

"This is just too funny," squealed the twins.

"I wish you had never come to this school, Grace," wailed Precious, burying her hands deep in her banana-colored curls.

Grace felt as if everything was in slow motion. The noise was almost deafening now. The squire was bellowing in her ear, and the crowd was shouting in confusion, trying to find out what was going on.

"Quiet, please," said Lady DuLac.

Suddenly the sound of a trumpet rang out across the field.

The crowd hushed. Grace turned, expecting to see a minstrel.

But it was Wilbur.

"Ladies and gentlemen, Your Royal Highnesses," he began. He was no longer swaying with dizziness, but his voice shook with nerves as he spoke. "I have something to explain."

CHAPTER SEVENTEEN
Happily Ever After...?

Wilbur bravely told the crowd of kings and queens how Grace had taken his place.

"She did it to help me and to make sure the joust could go ahead," he said.

When he had told the whole story, a hush fell over the field. The only sound was Grace's trembling knees as they clanked against the inside of her armor. It felt like the stunned silence would last forever.

But Lady DuLac stepped forward and took Grace by the hand.

Fairy Godmother Flint came striding across the grass too, her face solemn and thoughtful.

"I'm sorry I made such a mess of everything," whispered Grace. "I ruined the parade. My dress is ripped to shreds and . . ."

"Nonsense," said Lady DuLac. "I am very proud to have you representing Tall Towers today. You may not be standing here in front of us in the golden dress as we expected, but you have a trophy to prove you were a worthy choice to be our Golden Princess." Lady DuLac lifted the cup high in the air and the crowd cheered. "You rode with great talent and energy out there today. You showed courage and enthusiasm. But you also showed dignity and true grace."

"Really?" Grace's eyes opened wide in surprise. "All I did was knock things down."

"Ah," said Lady DuLac. "But you showed inner grace; that is what matters. A pretty curtsy is a useful thing for a royal girl to know how to do, but a *true* princess needs something deeper inside. That is what you showed us today, Grace. Although you yourself were very upset, you saw that Wilbur was in distress and you helped him. You did it for the good of everybody here. That is what *true* grace means."

Grace felt her cheeks blush. She couldn't believe Lady DuLac was talking about her. A worthy Golden Princess—it seemed impossible to believe.

But Flintheart held up her hand. "I have something to add," she announced.

Grace's heart banged like a hammer. *What was the strict fairy godmother going to say?*

"You also showed great elegance," said Flintheart warmly. Her stern face broke into a broad, happy smile—something Grace had never seen before. "Your back was as straight as a rod when you were riding out there."

Grace didn't want to say that a stiff suit of armor was a great help with that.

"Perhaps we should add jousting to your deportment class," roared Sir Rolling-Trot.

Grace giggled.

"I think that is going a little *too* far," said Flintheart. Her face was stony once more.

"AND *I* THINK WE SHOULD HAVE A LAP OF HONOR FROM OUR YOUNG PRINCESS," announced Squire Bellows.

Wilbur blew a fanfare on his trumpet.

The crowd cheered as Grace was lifted back onto Thunder. She could see her father leaping up and down with Pip on his shoulders.

"Well done, Grace! You were absolutely marvelous!" he roared.

Grace saw the shocked faces of Visalotta's parents, who were standing near him. Her aunt and uncle shook their heads. But she didn't care. So what if he was a little loud?

Why shouldn't Papa be excited? She was glad to make him proud.

"Just canter Thunder twice around the ring. That should do it," said Sir Rolling-Trot as she found her stirrups.

Grace and Thunder charged away.

They were beginning their second lap when Grace saw a blur of movement out of the corner of her eye. Something black and white was hurtling toward her.

Oh no, they've sent another knight to joust with me, she thought.

But as she turned, she saw it wasn't a knight charging across the ring. It was Billy.

He must have broken out of his stable.

He was galloping toward her, shaking his head at the giant horse and waving his horn like a lance.

He's jealous, thought Grace.

Billy charged forward and put his horn underneath her foot.

Bam!

The next thing Grace knew, she had clattered to the ground as Billy unseated her.

"You silly old thing," she said as he nuzzled her. "I loved riding Thunder, but I would never swap him for you."

Sir Rolling-Trot caught hold of Thunder, who was quaking with fear. Billy snorted at him.

The First Years—all except Precious—streamed onto the grass and helped Grace to her feet.

Even the twins joined in, patting Grace on the back and making her armor clang loudly. "That really was hilarious," they squealed.

"I don't think it made me or Billy look very elegant." Grace smiled as Scarlet and Izumi appeared beside her.

Grace's bun had come undone when Billy nuzzled her, and now her hair was flowing wildly down the back of her suit of armor.

"Jousting is so incredible," said Visalotta, pushing to the front of the group. Grace was amazed to see that her eyes were sparkling. She had never seen Visalotta excited about anything. "I'm going to ask for a suit of armor for my birthday!" she cried. She was leaping up and down now, and her whole face was bright and alive.

"Golly! I bet it will be made of solid gold," gasped the twins.

"I don't care if it's made from an old tin can." Visalotta shrugged. "I just want to have a go at jousting."

"Good for you," said Grace, putting her arm around Visalotta's shoulders, delighted that the princess had at last found something that made her happy.

"We should get Sir Rolling-Trot to teach us." Visalotta clapped.

"That's a wonderful idea," said Grace.

"We could have a school jousting club!" cried Princess Latisha. "With contests. It would be amazing."

"So you're not furious with me for ruining the parade?" asked Grace as she looked around at her classmates.

"Of course not," said Izumi.

"It wasn't even your fault," said Scarlet.

Grace knew her friends were just being kind. The whole parade had been spoiled the minute she tumbled down the steps.

"Of course it was my fault," she said. "You know how clumsy I am. I—"

"No." Scarlet opened her hand. "It really wasn't your fault. Look!"

"Pearls?" Grace stared at a little pile of loose beads in Scarlet's palm. "I don't understand."

"We found them on the steps. Right after you slipped," said Izumi.

"But those are Precious's pearls. The ones I broke," said Grace. "How did they . . . ? Oh . . ."

Suddenly everything made sense. Grace remembered how her feet had felt as if they were rolling away from underneath her.

"Precious said she was going to teach you a lesson," Visalotta said. "She was very excited about something all last night."

"I think she must have put the pearls on the steps deliberately," said Izumi. "To make sure you would trip."

"How absolutely rotten," gasped the twins. And for once they did look truly shocked.

"She was jealous you were the Golden Princess," said Scarlet. "Precious wanted to make you look foolish even if it meant risking her valuable pearls."

"But her plan didn't quite work, did it?" said a stern voice.

The First Years looked round to see Fairy Godmother Flint standing behind them. Her eyes were flashing with anger.

"I'll take those," she said, holding out her hand for the pearls. "Now, if you will excuse me, I need to have a word with Princess Precious."

As the kings and queens climbed into their royal boats, ready to sail away for the holidays, twelve First Year princesses lingered on the shore for a moment before they joined them.

"It really has been a wonderful term, hasn't it?" said Grace.

"I almost wish it wasn't the holidays," said Visalotta.

"I'm going to miss Beauty," said Scarlet. "Who'd have thought I was scared of unicorns just a few weeks ago."

Grace smiled. She was going to miss Billy too. She had tucked him into his stable with a bowl of fresh peaches and made Sir

Rolling-Trot promise to let him out into the meadow every day.

"Hold on a minute," said Princess Emmeline. "There are only twelve of us here. Who's missing?"

"Precious," said Princess Latisha. "Old Flintheart was absolutely furious about the horrible trick she played with the pearls. Precious isn't allowed to go home until she has scooped up all the poop in Silver Meadow."

"Golly," squealed the twins. "That really isn't a very princessy job."

"And there's going to be a lot of poop from all that jousting," said Grace.

She looked across the harbor and saw her aunt and uncle pacing impatiently on the deck of their speedboat.

The clouds looked heavy now, and a large white snowflake fluttered down toward them.

"I had better get going," said Scarlet. "My parents are giving Wilbur a lift in our boat. I don't want to make him late for the Royal Musicians Academy."

"Have a wonderful holiday," said Grace, hugging Scarlet and Izumi tightly. "See you next term for more fun in Sky Dorm."

The girls hurried away toward their parents.

"Ready to go home, brave Sir Grace?" chuckled her father, bowing.

"Yes." Grace smiled. "Although I wish I'd gotten to keep the suit of armor." She had given it back to Squire Bellows and was wearing her pretty school pinafore and blue sash.

"You're a proper princess now," said Pip as Grace climbed into their little wooden rowing boat.

"Do you know what? I really think I am," said Grace. And she gave her sister her best, most princessy curtsy.

But as she tried to stand straight, the boat rocked beneath her.

"Whoops!" she cried. She flung out her arms to steady herself . . . but it was too late.

She toppled over and fell into the sea.

Splosh!

Are there dragons at Tall Towers Academy?

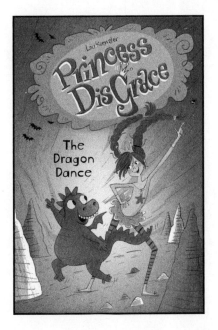

Read on for a sneak peek at Grace's next adventure!

It was Friday, when the princesses were allowed to ride their unicorns for an hour after school. As soon as class was over, Grace had grabbed her binoculars and dashed to the stables. She hadn't stopped to find a proper rope . . . or even a saddle. She'd left Billy in his halter and ridden him bareback along the beach at a gallop.

Ambling back to school along the high cliff path, she'd spotted a perfect lookout tree. Hundreds of birds were swooping about the cliffs, searching for the best place to make their spring nests.

But it wasn't birds that Grace was interested in.

"Who's up there? What are you doing?"

said a sharp voice from beneath the tree.

Grace looked down through the branches and saw the school gamekeeper with a crossbow slung across his back. His tiny niece, Hetty, stood just behind him.

"Oh. It's you, Princess Grace." The keeper sighed. "I should have guessed." Keeper Falcon was a mean-looking man with narrow eyes and quick movements like a fox's. He always seemed to find Grace in the wrong place at the wrong time.

"Hello up there!" Young Hetty waved. The little girl could not have been more different from her uncle. She had a round, open face, with big, wide eyes and a sprinkling of freckles across her nose.

"I love your unicorn. Can I pet him?" she asked.

"Of course," said Grace. "His name's Billy. Give him a really good scratch behind the ears. He loves that."

But Keeper Falcon coughed and nudged his niece fiercely. "Where are your manners, Hetty?" he growled.

"Sorry." Hetty blushed and dropped to one knee in a deep curtsy. "Good afternoon, Your Majesty. I hope you are having a pleasant day."

"Very pleasant." Grace smiled. "But you don't need to curtsy to me." It seemed ridiculous. The little girl was a year or so older than Grace's own sister, Princess Pip. Just like Pip, she clearly wished she had a unicorn of her own.

I know how that feels, thought Grace. Until she had come to Tall Towers last term, having her own unicorn was all she had ever dreamed of too.

"Go ahead," she said. "Pet Billy as much as you like."

"That's very kind of you. But Hetty must know her place," said the gamekeeper with a stiff bow. "She is lucky to live with me now that her poor mother is dead. Your kind headmistress, Lady Du Lac, is generous enough to let her stay here on Coronet Island. It's Hetty's job to help me with the chores."

"Like feeding the peacocks and doves," said Hetty brightly.

"But you must remember that you are a servant, Hetty. Not a royal princess like the other girls," the keeper barked.

At the harsh tone of his voice, Hetty jumped backward as if she had been slapped.

"Sorry, Uncle," she murmured. "I just wanted to pet the unicorn, that's all."

"Well, mind your manners," snapped the keeper. Grace was shocked at how strict he was. He bowed again as he turned back toward her. "Are you bird-watching up there, Young Majesty?"

"No. It's not birds I'm looking out for," said Grace, dropping down to a lower branch. "It's dragons."